HOLD LOVE TIGHTLY

Megan Lane

A CANDLELIGHT ECSTASY ROMANCE ®

Published by
Dell Publishing Co., Inc.
1 Dag Hammarskjold Plaza
New York, New York 10017

Dell ® TM 681510, Dell Publishing Co., Inc.

Candlelight Ecstasy Romance®, 1,203,540, is a registered
trademark of Dell Publishing Co., Inc.,
New York, New York.

ISBN: 0–440–13676–8

Printed in the United States of America
First printing—September 1983

A Candlelight Ecstasy Romance®

**"WHERE DO WE GO FROM HERE, BROCK?"
THE QUESTION SET A FRIGHTENINGLY
DISTURBING PULSE BEATING AT HER
TEMPLES.**

Kneeling down before the fire, Brock stared into the dancing flames for what seemed to Jenna an eternity. "What do you think, Jen? Shall we try again? I'm sure you know it won't be easy. We've got to change, you and I—if we haven't already. The jealousy, the possessivness, the competitivness—they'll destroy us if we let them. And it's not easy trying to make a new life for myself. My music was so much a part of me for so long. . . . I won't settle for less from myself because of my hand. I won't be weaker because of it. I've got to find my own way."

She nodded, but she couldn't help but wonder if he was asking too much of himself. Why couldn't he let her help him? Was he still too proud to admit he couldn't do it all alone? But she didn't say those things, because he wasn't ready to listen. And they were too close to finally rediscovering what they'd lost.

A CANDLELIGHT ECSTASY ROMANCE ®

To Our Readers:

We have been delighted with your enthusiastic response to Candlelight Ecstasy Romances®, and we thank you for the interest you have shown in this exciting series.

In the upcoming months we will continue to present the distinctive sensuous love stories you have come to expect only from Ecstasy. We look forward to bringing you many more books from your favorite authors and also the very finest work from new authors of contemporary romantic fiction.

As always, we are striving to present the unique, absorbing love stories that you enjoy most—books that are more than ordinary romance.

Your suggestions and comments are always welcome. Please write to us at the address below.

Sincerely,

The Editors
Candlelight Romances
1 Dag Hammarskjold Plaza
New York, New York 10017

CHAPTER ONE

Jenna O'Neil lightly strummed the strings of her guitar, and her rich alto voice deepened, stroking the audience with its velvet softness.

Closing her deep brown eyes against the brightness of the single spotlight shining down on her, she prevented even the most perceptive observer from seeing the glittering sheen reflecting the pain of her aching heart. The song she was singing had been Brock's favorite, one he had written for her. The words lingered in her ears after she had sung them, and she told herself for the thousandth time that she should have had better sense than to become involved with Brock. A musician married to a musician.

She had known it wouldn't work the first time Brock Hanson asked her out to an early-morning breakfast, but she had never dreamed of the heartache, the turmoil, he would wreak inside her, creating turbulence that couldn't be calmed or soothed no matter how far or how long she ran.

The resounding applause brought her thoughts sharply back to the present, back to the exclusive nightclub and the capacity crowd. She opened her eyes and smiled warmly at her audience, her response natural and easy.

"Give us another song, Jenna," a tall jovial man seated in front of the stage urged, using her name as familiarly as if he knew her personally. "I've come all the way to Boston from Jacksonville, Florida, just to hear you sing and play."

11

And to look at me, Jenna thought in amusement, noting the way the man's eyes lingered on the cleft of her breasts, tantalizingly exposed in the clinging fuchsia dress. Her clothing had been one of the things Brock had complained most bitterly about once they had gotten married. Suddenly he had wanted no one to see her but him, and he knew as well as she that in this business a woman needed to look her most alluring.

She tried harder to give her attention to the man in front of her instead of to the one in her past, but it was a futile effort. It always had been. Brock had been the dominant force in her life ever since she had met him. He had been part of the orchestra that accompanied her on her first album, and when they had been introduced by a mutual friend at a party later, she had been instantly attracted to him. They had spoken briefly, then circulated, but she had been acutely aware of him watching her, and she had been strangely nervous under his penetrating appraisal.

She could still see those blue eyes now as clearly as she had then. And it had been two years. Two years since she had first met him, eleven months since she had last seen him. Their whirlwind courtship had lasted twelve days, their marriage thirteen months. Unlucky thirteen, Jenna told herself.

She and Brock had been known in intimate circles and to the media alike as the music world's most beautiful—and most explosive—new couple. Brock's blond handsomeness was as startling as her own dark beauty, and as a pair they were stunningly attractive.

"Sing 'Hold Love Tightly' just once more," the man insisted, his loud voice carrying and causing others in the audience to echo his enthusiasm.

Jenna's full rosy lips curved sensually, and she murmured in a tone which said that the man was the most important person in the world at the moment, "I'd love to do them all for you tonight, but Dan wants to close, and the band wants to go home. You've been a wonderful audience, and I hope you'll all come back again."

12

Standing up, she smoothed down the shimmering gown, her hands tracing her curvaceous hips and attracting more than one male gaze. Her movements were unconsciously seductive; she was a beautiful woman, her figure voluptuous, her bearing regal, her five-feet-ten-inch height giving her presence. At twenty-eight she was at her loveliest. She knew she was attractive, but there was none of the arrogance in her that often went with that knowledge.

"Just once more," the fan requested, but Jenna had learned how to be firm long ago—with everyone but Brock.

"You're sweet, and I'm very flattered, but you don't want me to lose my job, do you? I have to abide by the boss's rules." It was a lie, of course; Dan was a personal friend. She played in his night spot because of her friendship with him and because Boston was her home. She was eagerly sought after by all the local clubs. Her first album had been a big hit, and her second album, on which "Hold Love Tightly" was the lead, had been a tremendous success, causing her career to soar to unimagined heights. "Hold Love Tightly" had been in the top ten on the charts for many weeks, propelling Jenna into fame and fortune.

She scanned the room, looking for Dan. The band began playing their theme song, which was Dan's cue to help Jenna from the stage and invite the customers to have one last drink. Her breath caught in her throat when she glanced at the exit. For a moment, a single crazy moment, she thought she had seen Brock leaning against the doorway. She knew that was absurd, but her gaze swept the rest of the room, then moved swiftly in the direction of the door again, seeking the tall blond man with the moody blue eyes and sensitive face. Her breath escaped in a disappointed sigh; she had imagined him, of course. He wasn't there. No one was.

She blew a kiss to the audience and, her guitar in hand, began to walk away despite the pleas to sing another song. Dan rushed up beside her as people began to clap and shout "Encore!"

"Give her a big hand, ladies and gentlemen. Jenna O'Neil."

Smiling at Dan over her shoulder, Jenna slipped off the stage. The audience, obeying him as always, applauded energetically. Dan had a way of sounding very final, and once he put in an appearance, the crowd seemed to know it was useless to ask for more songs. His six-feet-four height, square build, and craggy features were deterrents to further requests. He made his announcement for last bar call, then followed Jenna to her small dressing room.

He closed the door just as Jenna dropped down on a soft gold couch and pulled her high-heeled shoes off. His glance raked longingly over the brief display of trim ankles and shapely legs. A frown caused him to look rougher than usual, and he eased his bulky frame onto the dainty chair, turning it around so that he could rest thick arms on its back.

"The damnedest thing just happened," he told her, his powerful voice revealing surprise. "I could have sworn that I saw Brock in the doorway just before you went off. That's why I was delayed a minute. I went to the exit, but there was no one there."

Jenna licked her full lower lip. It couldn't be: Brock wouldn't come back into her life now. Not after all this time. Her laughter was brittle. "That *is* the damnedest thing. I thought I saw him too. A ghost, I suppose."

Her tongue almost tripped over the words. Brock had vanished from the life they knew as surely as if he had been killed; he had gone away on a gig for a weekend, and Jenna had never seen him again. Not that she should have, she reminded herself tormentedly. She and Brock had split up several days before that, and she had known that reconciliation was impossible.

He had been too explosive and she too vulnerable to his outbursts. He had been jealous of the attention men gave her, and she of the attention he gave women. Their careers had also been a source of constant conflict. The two had followed different musical paths, and she had had the first record out. Their last devastating quarrel reverberated harshly in her ears, and she winced. Why was she always going over the past?

14

"I swear I think it was Brock," Dan said. "But he was different somehow. I sensed it more than saw it. He was standing in the dark, in the shadows, you know, like he didn't want anyone to see him."

Jenna felt a sudden rush of tears at the back of her eyes and throat. How she had longed to see Brock again. No one else would ever do. She had dated—most seriously with Dan—but Brock had haunted her. Not only had *she* not seen him again, neither had anyone else. He seemed to have abandoned not just her but his career as well. Of course there were hundreds of clubs he could be playing in here and abroad; however, none of the crowd seemed to know his whereabouts either, unless, Jenna thought resentfully, Brock had told them not to tell her. Still, in a business like this, word generally got around sooner or later. Everyone sensed that this wasn't the usual break a musician took when he needed to rejuvenate himself.

For weeks Jenna had been terrified that Brock had died in some dreadful accident or been struck down by some deadly disease, but finally he had had his mother give Jenna a message telling her where to send the last of his personal belongings. Jenna had tried to deliver them herself, but no one had answered the door, and when she had gone back to the address later, the apartment had been vacated.

Then she had known that Brock never meant to see her again. Ever. How she had cried that night, as if she had no life without him. But she had survived, somehow. She had become even more successful. The pain and the glory of loving Brock had given her songs new dimension, her talent new intensity, her delivery new depth.

Brushing at the glossy length of black hair that cloaked her shoulders, Jenna murmured resolutely, "It wasn't Brock." Her rich brown eyes met Dan's dark gaze. "I'm tired, Dan. Please call me a cab. I'm going home."

"Let me drive you," he coaxed. "We'll stop for coffee."

She shook her head. "Thanks, but not tonight." Her eyes were

15

suddenly serious. "I've given you the four days I promised you, Dan, and now I'm going to take some time off. My album has been wrapped up, and I've finished all the commitments I've been booked for. I'm simply exhausted. I don't want to hear anything about city-to-city tours or Las Vegas bookings. I'm going to Prout's Neck and spend a couple of months there just unwinding."

"But it'll be dead there," Dan retorted. "It's October, and the season is almost over. Everyone is going back home."

She smiled and nodded. "I know. That's exactly what I'm counting on. No tourists. No gawkers. No crowds. Just me and a few of the year-rounders. It will be heavenly."

Dan shook his head. "I don't think so, Jenna. You're a social animal. You love people. You'll be bored to tears. You know you hate it in the fall and winter. Besides, what will you do there? Who will you talk to?"

"Myself," she murmured. "I'll get in touch with myself. Ever since my album made the top ten, I've been on the go promoting it. I can't keep up this pace. I need some time to myself." *Some time to get off the merry-go-round long enough to get over Brock,* she wanted to add, but she had too much pride to voice such thoughts.

"I'll give you a week," Dan said gruffly. "Prout's Neck isn't for you when there's no one around. Besides," he added, "I don't like the thought of you being there all alone in that big house. These are crazy times, and you're a personality."

"And what's a personality?" she asked, laughing teasingly. But she was pleased by his concern. "I'll be just fine. Anyway, the Millets still live there." Actually they had been Brock's close friends, but Jenna had kept in touch with them.

A smile softened Dan's hard features. "I'm sure you will be," he agreed, "but I'll miss you. I can come and see you, can't I?"

Jenna's eyes twinkled with merriment. "Oh, I suppose so," she teased. "As long as you behave yourself."

Laughing huskily, Dan stood up and walked over to sit beside

16

her. When he drew her into his arms and hugged her, Jenna shook her head. "You don't know how to behave yourself," she joked.

She enjoyed Dan's company, and he was the only person in the world who knew how she struggled with her artist's temperament, swinging from highs to lows with no conceivable explanation. She felt comfortable with him, secure in the knowledge that he would be there if she needed him. The ten years that separated them in age were insignificant, for they knew each other well and had for many years. And he knew about Brock. Yes, she would enjoy a visit from him, but she ruefully admitted to herself that a visit was all it would be.

She could never fall in love with Dan, and she was afraid that was what he hoped for. She wasn't one of those women who would pine away for years over a love that had gone wrong, but she was very much afraid that it would be a long, long time—if ever—before she was sufficiently over Brock to risk giving her heart away again.

"I need that cab," she told Dan softly. "I want to go home."

He nodded, and without another word he went to the phone.

Jenna stared at the city lights as the cab worked its way along the twisting, narrow streets of Beacon Hill. Generally she never tired of the red brick sidewalks, gaslight lamps, and pretty flowers in the window boxes, but tonight her mind was filled with other things. It was almost 2 A.M., and the traffic was light. She sighed unhappily as the car stopped in front of the old vine-covered brownstone which she loved so well.

When she had paid the driver, she walked quickly up the steps, inserted her key, and entered her elegant living room. It had the finest furnishings money could buy, and it had been decorated by one of the city's best-known interior decorators. Yes, Jenna mused as she glanced absently around her, the days when she had struggled for every penny and envied the people who lived on the Hill were long gone. Money was no object now, but

17

money couldn't buy her what she sorely wanted, and money couldn't keep back the lonely nights and the haunting memories.

Oblivious to the beauty around her, she went down the hall to the bedroom and slipped out of her gown. She pulled on a flowered caftan and returned to the living room to pour herself a glass of white wine at the rich dark-wood bar. Sipping the wine, she wandered around the plush room, trying to unwind after the performance so that she could sleep. Finally she settled down on the long beige couch, swung her legs up over the back, and listened to the messages on her answering machine, knowing that there would be at least one, maybe two, from her mother.

The phone rang while Jenna listened to the messages, and she picked it up with a startled "Hello." She was surprised that someone would phone this late, even though many people knew she would still be up. "Hello," she repeated, annoyed that she hadn't gotten a response. Abruptly the party on the other end hung up.

"Damn," Jenna muttered before she, too, slammed the phone down. Her nerves were so tautly strung tonight that she would have welcomed someone to talk to. She thought briefly of the caller; it wasn't the first time this had happened recently, which made her feel just a little uneasy. But she didn't allow herself to speculate. Someone had probably just dialed wrong or had the wrong number, she guessed.

She got up and stood looking at the phone for a moment while she drank the last of her wine. Then she took a quick shower before snuggling down loving the free, unconfined feeling of sleeping naked.

She closed her eyes, but she couldn't sleep. Brock. Brock. Tormenting. Disturbing. And always she asked herself the same question: If Brock had loved her as he had maintained, how could he have disappeared from her life, never even to speak to her again? She would give all that she owned for one more chance to talk to him, to try to recapture what they had shared— the joy and the misery of their love.

She remembered the last time they were together in familiar haunting detail. Jenna had gone to the nightclub where Brock was playing, and she had arrived in time to see him sharing a drink with a gorgeous blonde. She had been angry with him that night not particularly because of the woman—she knew that a performer was expected to be friendly with the patrons—but because of Brock's attitude and the game they were playing. He had been to her club the previous night and had become angry because a man was openly ogling her as she sat before him in a dress Brock had forbidden her to wear.

If only he hadn't *forbidden*, she thought for the thousandth time. If only Brock had learned to ask instead of demand, but that had never been his way. He was used to giving orders and being obeyed. Jenna shook her head, wishing she could take back the angry words she had uttered, wishing she could wipe that ugly night from their lives, wishing she could apologize to Brock.

They had quarreled all the way home about her career and his, and in a moment of fury she had cried, "You're jealous of me, jealous because I have the first record, because my career is moving faster than yours, and because of all the attention I get!"

The statement had been calculated to wound; she had known he was sensitive because he hadn't yet had the success they both had been striving for. His goals were set: He wanted to succeed both as a song writer and a piano player. He was superb at both, but his time simply hadn't come yet. It had been inexcusable of Jenna to make the statement: her success wouldn't have come so easily without his encouragement and support. And still the knowledge hadn't kept her from accusing Brock of being jealous because he hadn't achieved her position on the career ladder.

She hadn't honestly thought it, of course, and she hadn't meant it. She had known that her words would reach a vulnerable spot within him, and that's why she had uttered them. She had often wondered why it was that when someone knew a person intimately enough to be familiar with his weaknesses, he used that knowledge to do the most damage.

19

In her case it had been a grave error, the coup de grace of their stormy relationship. She could still hear Brock's sharp response. "Do you *really* mean that? Do you honestly think that I don't want you to succeed?"

"Yes," she had foolishly flung back at him, knowing it would wound him and wanting it to. "Yes, I do think so."

Brock had closed up on her then in that cruel, absolute way of his. She had known that there would be no more conversation until he relented and opened up to her again. It had been one of the things she had hated most about him, the way he had of shutting her out.

They had slept in the same bed that night, but there had been none of the closeness, the loving, the apologies that usually came. She had yearned for his touch, but she had had too much pride to approach him first. He had lain silent and rigid at her side, nursing his bruised ego while she cursed her silly tongue.

Finally they both had gone to sleep without a word, but Jenna had promised herself that she would have a discussion with Brock and clear the air. Her words had been spoken in anger and haste. She had to make him understand how much she respected his talent and that she knew in her heart he was happy for her sucess.

It hadn't been necessary to deliver her well-planned speech. Brock had left Jenna the next day. While she was grocery shopping he had packed his belongings and moved out. She had returned to find him gone, and she had wanted to die. Actually die. In that first awful moment when she had realized that he had really gone, she had been too stunned to be rational. The arguments, the pain, the tension, had been inconsequential compared to the prospect of never again knowing Brock's loving, glowing under the praise in his eyes, sharing a special moment with him, hearing his husky laughter.

And then had come the incredulity. He had *left* her! Just like that, he had walked out on her. It didn't seem possible. But then, she hadn't honestly believed that Brock wouldn't come back to her. They had had problems, sure, but who didn't? And they had loved each other. At least she had loved him, and she had been reasonably sure that he loved her. But he hadn't come back. He hadn't even called. Jenna told herself that she didn't need him, didn't want him with the pain that was an inevitable part of him, but it was a lie.

When she lay in her bed—their bed—all alone, counting the dark hours, listening for the familiar sound of Brock's footsteps, she ached for him to come and hold her again. But he hadn't returned. Finally the call had come from his mother, adding to the humiliation Jenna had felt at his sudden departure.

By then she would have gone to him on her knees and apologized, for she had apparently hurt him more deeply than she had ever dreamed possible. An even more horrible idea nagged at the raw edges of her mind. Had Brock found that he didn't love her after all? Had he realized he had made a mistake in marrying her and been glad for some final confrontation explosive enough to give him cause to leave?

She shook her head. No, that couldn't be; he couldn't have not loved her when she had loved him so deeply. Still loved him so deeply.

Abruptly she flung aside the sheet and went back to the living room for a second glass of wine. She needed sleep desperately. She filled her glass, then switched on the television, staring at the screen as she drank the wine, needing the distraction but not really seeing what was playing. Restless, she soon flipped the set off, then trailed back to her bedroom. And at last sleep wooed her deep into the blackness of her mind.

The insistent, bothersome ring of the phone penetrated Jenna's sleep, awakening her. Reaching out to grasp the receiver, she mumbled sleepily, "Hello."

"Jenna! Jenna, is that you?"

At the sound of her mother's voice Jenna rolled over on her back and brushed at the tumbled dark masses of her hair. She stretched and tried to rouse herself fully so that she could deal with Joan O'Neil calmly. "Yes, Mother."

"Jenna, I've been worried about you. Why didn't you call me yesterday? You know how concerned I am for your safety since that actress was attacked."

Jenna was reminded of the mighty battle she had fought to separate her life from her mother's after she finished college; she knew the break had never been clean. Her mother meant well, but she had always been too possessive, too wrapped up in her only daughter. Jenna's father had died when she was too small to even remember him, so all her life it had been just herself and her mother.

Mr. O'Neil had left a modest inheritance, which helped them survive, and Joan had taken a job as a clerk in a clothing store. Times had been hard, and the two of them had clung together through the years while Jenna's mother ensured that her daughter's life would be easier in the future. Jenna knew that she owed Joan a lot.

Sighing in resignation, she replied patiently, "I didn't have a chance. You know how busy I've been." Before the woman could start in again, Jenna reminded her, "Mother, I'm twenty-eight. I love you, and I do appreciate your concern, but you don't have any cause for this excessive worry. Really, I'll be just fine. I can take care of myself."

She should have known what was coming before her mother spoke again. "Just like when you married that—that piano player. I told you it wouldn't work. Real love doesn't happen like that, and you know if you had listened to me—"

"Mother, let's not go through it all again," Jenna interrupted firmly. She knew well how her mother felt about Brock, and she didn't want to be reminded of it at the moment. Joan's opposition to Jenna's marriage had hurt her deeply and almost broken the loving bond between them. "But I am glad you called. I wanted to tell you that I'm going to Prout's Neck for a couple of months. I'll be at the house there the entire time. You can

22

reach me if you need me by calling the Millets. They'll be glad to give me the message, I'm sure. You still have their number, don't you?"

"Yes, Jenna, but I don't understand. Why are you going there?"

"I need a rest. I'm exhausted."

"But *there,* Jenna—"

"Yes, now, don't forget to call the Millets if you need me. I'll see you in a couple of months. 'Bye, Mother."

" 'Bye."

Jenna had to smile as she replaced the phone. For once her mother had been too stunned to argue against Jenna's plans. Slipping back under the covers for a few more luxurious minutes, she refused to give her mother the power to make her feel guilty because she hadn't listened to another of her admonitions. She had dealt with all those emotions before too. She sighed raggedly. She really did need a rest, and she could certainly get it at Prout's Neck. There wasn't even a phone in the house, she reminded herself blissfully.

Glancing at the clock, she saw that it was only eight; she was still weary, but all of a sudden she began to feel a surge of excitement. She had been to the house only once since she and Brock had split up, and even though it had been glorious summer, she had been too depressed to stay.

Now she was eager for the solitude and warmth of the sprawling structure. It had been an extravagance she had insisted they couldn't afford when they bought it, but Brock had convinced her that with both their incomes it wouldn't be a problem. Of course he had been right; the money she had earned from the first album had been beyond her wildest dreams, and the money she was earning from her second was even more impressive.

Yes, she was looking forward to Prout's Neck. It would be beautiful at this time of year, as was all of New England. The fierce cold would come in a matter of weeks, maybe even days, as unpredictable as New England's weather was, but now fall's touch was everywhere, splashing the trees with splendid color, making the air crisp and invigorating, the starry evenings brisk, perfect for after-dinner walks.

Suddenly Jenna leaped out of bed and raced to the kitchen to make herself a cup of coffee, as if every single moment she delayed were important. Within an hour she had dressed in cranberry-colored slacks, matching pullover sweater, and loafers, and having packed the car with odds and ends and her guitar, she was on her way up north to the craggy coast of Maine.

As she left Boston's diversely delightful blend of new and old behind, the area became more rural, less congested. Massachusetts gave way to Maine's magnificent rocky seacoast, and Jenna enjoyed the glorious views before her. The brooding, dark rock-strewn coastline had always excited her.

She grew increasingly eager to reach her destination as she left mile after mile behind and finally turned onto the winding road leading to Prout's Neck. When she saw the Black Point Inn, she knew she was home. Home, she told herself. What an odd word to choose. She and Brock hadn't really referred to this place as home. Prout's Neck was a vacation spot made famous by East Coast socialites, and the number of tourists flocking to it to enjoy the stunning beaches, scenic beauty, tennis courts, golf links, and country and yacht clubs grew each year. Like the others, Jenna had fallen in love with the Neck the first time she had seen it. She especially loved the rustic, weathered beauty of the Black Point Inn, and she and Brock had enjoyed many sumptuous meals there.

Their house was a vacation retreat, as were most of the others in the area. Brock had known a number of the regulars and the summer residents, and while he and Jenna kept to themselves as much as they socialized when they were here, they had especially liked the company of the Millets.

She smiled, remembering some of the good times the four of them had shared here. Martha Millet was fifteen years younger than her husband, but she was a lot older in outlook than Evan. He was low-key, easygoing, shrugging off responsibility to indulge in his painting; he was fortunate to be a well-known artist and to have Martha to take care of the necessary details of life, like washing clothes and cooking, Jenna thought with a smile.

Sometimes Evan didn't know day from night, and Jenna and Martha had once spent a day together and purposely not called Evan to lunch or dinner to see if the man even felt hunger when he was lost in his other world. To their amazement they discovered that he didn't. He never came out of his studio, and finally they could stand it no more and were forced to take food in to him.

Jenna sighed contentedly. Yes, she would love to see them again. It had been too long. She had called, but that wasn't the same, and on the phone Martha had seemed remote. Suddenly it occurred to her that perhaps Martha was distant toward her now.

After all, the couple had been Brock's friends. He had known them for years before Jenna had been introduced to them. But she dismissed the idea before it could grow. She and Martha had kindred souls; Martha wasn't the kind to play those games. She wouldn't have turned on either partner after the marriage went sour.

Jenna winced at the term. *Fell apart* was more appropriate. *Dissolved. Ended.* As she drove down by the water she gazed out at the blue expanse beyond the rocky border, and her mind was filled with a thousand memories of Brock and herself together. When she drove up the road, she encountered the chain fence which marked the residential area, notifying the vast number of summer visitors who wandered all over Prout's Neck that this area was private.

She stopped her car and used her key to open the padlock so she could enter, and her melancholy thoughts gave way to rising excitement. She had avoided coming here because she was sure

25

the house would remind her too much of Brock, but inexplicably she felt that this was where she belonged.

The road wove back into the woods, working its way beneath the flaming brightness of gloriously colored leaves, and Jenna found herself driving more rapidly. There it was, at the end of the long winding drive, the house she and Brock had so affectionately and unimaginatively named Solace. She smiled, thinking what a pity it was that two musicians couldn't have thought up something more original, more romantic.

For a moment she gazed at the two-story gray clapboard house nestled under the towering branches of two ancient elm trees. They had chosen this particular house because the view of the water was breathtaking. Now that she was here, Jenna stared at the house, oddly reluctant to enter. Telling herself that she was being silly, she left the car and strolled up the walkway, not even taking her purse with her.

A breeze tugged at her hair, dragging it across her face. When Jenna raised her hand to her cheek, she saw that her fingers were trembling. A few bright leaves fluttered across the porch, and memories began to tumble through Jenna's mind, stirring up disturbing emotions.

Inserting her key, she eased the door open with the anticipation of a child opening a present. She wanted to savor her first glimpse of the home where she and Brock had shared so many treasured times. She was so excited about being here that she actually imagined she could smell the rich aroma of coffee, and even a teasing hint of gardenia scent.

She glanced down the hall, noting the brillance of the colors in the Oriental rug that covered the floor. Then she walked over to the living room and peered in, recalling how she and Brock had decorated this house with such pleasure, choosing only the pieces they were wild about.

She stopped short, stunned by the sight before her. Her breath caught in her throat, and she felt as though surely her heart had stopped beating, despite the blood pounding so furiously at her temples. "Brock!"

It seemed to her that she had shrieked the name, but in actuality she had murmured it so quietly that it was little more than a whisper. Brock was here! The blond husband she had thought about so intensely and so hauntingly since last night was before her, as if he had materialized out of her want and need for him.

Brock looked up as though he had sensed her presence; their gazes clashed, and in that single second before his blue eyes became hard and cold, Jenna knew that he hadn't forgotten her any more than she had forgotten him.

"Jenna," he murmured huskily, the word almost a groan as a frown marred his handsome features.

Jenna's attention was distracted from his eyes, and she realized that something wasn't right. In her surprise at seeing him she hadn't really looked at anything but those blue eyes, which had always had the power to hypnotize her. Her hands flew to her mouth, and she recoiled as her gaze raked over Brock's face, tracing those familiar sensuous details. A thin jagged scar ran along the length of his left cheek and down into his mouth; it twisted in its route so that it cut across his upper lip, crossing the cupid's bow Jenna had always thought so beautifully formed.

When Jenna's eyes returned to his, she saw that he was glowering at her hostilely. Then he looked away, and she saw that a petite, shapely blonde shared the couch with him. Of course she hadn't honestly expected him to remain celibate, but to see him here, and with this woman, after all the long months, was a devastating blow. The woman was holding one of Brock's hands, and Jenna was appalled by the bitter reactions churning within her.

Her heart was thundering in her ears, and her legs were rebelliously near failing her. So incoherent were her thoughts that she was unable to speak. She needed time to marshal her defenses, and all she wanted was to put distance between herself and the sight of Brock with this woman.

"Excuse me," she mumbled inadequately. Then she turned on her heel and ran headlong back to the car, trampling and scattering the red and gold leaves which lay in piles at her feet. They seemed to mock her as they winked and glittered in the bright sunlight which spilled through the dancing leaves that still clung to the overhead branches of the elms.

CHAPTER TWO

Brock stared after the tall, dark beauty in shocked silence. He had been a fool to come here, but he had never dreamed that Jenna would turn up. She hadn't cared for Prout's Neck much in the fall and winter, when most of the summer residents had gone home. Even Martha had agreed that this was the last place Jenna would be.

Running his hands through his thick blond hair, he cursed bitterly to himself. He was just beginning to see daylight in the mess he had made of his life. He was even writing again. He had roamed the coast for months, looking for he didn't know what. And he had known an aching need to return here, although he wasn't quite sure why. He had been pulled back by invisible chains—chains he knew he could never break until he learned why they shackled him.

He had always found peace at Prout's Neck; his family had come here when he was a child, and he would stand gazing out to sea as men had done for untold years before him. The sea held secrets of time and place, and Brock could put things in perspective when he studied it.

"Who was that woman?"

He turned to look at the small, pretty woman beside him. The slanting rays of sun filtered through the bay window to scatter rich gold over her hair. She was appealing; he had thought that before. But she wasn't Jenna.

"She was my wife," he told her.

* * *

Jenna was shaking all over when she got into the car, and she started it without thought. Throwing it into reverse, she backed out of the driveway and onto the road. Then she headed blindly in the other direction, still not believing what she had seen. Brock! Brock and that woman! Brock and those scars!

She was actually gasping for breath, and at last she collected her wits about her enough to pull off to the side of the road before she did something dangerous to herself or someone else.

She had been astonished to see Brock sitting there before her. What was he doing here? What had happened to his face? Who was that woman? Had the Millets known he was here?

Of course they had, she told herself bitterly. They had known, and they hadn't told her. She was overwhelmed by the barrage of questions flooding her mind, and she was still shaking from the unexpectedness of seeing Brock after so long.

The Millets had answers to her questions; she was sure of it. And she needed those answers before she confronted Brock again, as she knew she would have to.

Turning the car around, she worked her way deeper into the maze of the houses. Her pulse still hadn't slowed when she pulled up before a neat two-story white clapboard house shuttered in green, partially hidden behind mammoth hedges.

Somehow she made it to the door and knocked with a trembling hand. When Martha answered, Jenna was rigidly immobile, in spite of the anger and the disappointment gnawing at her insides.

"Jenna! It's been ages." The sparkle in those warm gray eyes suddenly vanished in the face of Jenna's obvious distress. Jenna saw the generous smile fade as quickly as it had come.

"I want to know about Brock," Jenna said simply, the statement in no way conveying what she was feeling.

Martha pressed her lips together, and Jenna could see the guilt written on the other woman's face as plainly as if Evan had painted it there in vivid colors. "Yes," Martha said, the slight quiver in her voice betraying her anxiety and discomfort. "Yes, of course you do. Come on in."

Stepping into the house on quaking legs, Jenna followed Martha, only vaguely aware of the tense posture of the woman in front of her. Jenna's eyes appraised familiar rooms as Martha led her through the house and back to the country kitchen; here they had spent hours talking and laughing in the homey atmosphere of hanging pots and pans, colorful gourds and dried pods, and a profusion of Evan's seascapes.

Martha indicated one of the big, comfortable chairs surrounding an antique oak table placed near a massive open fireplace that had often kept winter's chill at bay for the occupants of the house. Today Martha rubbed her arms, although there was neither fire nor winter's chill to affect her, and Jenna noted her friend's unease. She could barely contain the thoughts spinning around in circles inside her head, beating at the edges of her mind, demanding solutions.

Although Martha went to put on a pot of coffee, Jenna couldn't even wait for that comfort to ease her distress. "You must know that Brock's at Solace."

Martha whirled around to face Jenna, her cheeks flaming brightly. "Yes, we know. He's been there several weeks."

"What happened to him? Where has he been? What caused that scar on his face?"

"He was in an accident," Martha answered, her brow wrinkling.

"An accident?" Jenna repeated. "When? Oh, Martha, how could you not have told me?" she asked, her feeling of betrayal evident in every accusing word.

Taking two thick mugs from the mahogany cupboard, Martha seemed to be playing for time, struggling for words before she brought the cups to the table with her. "We had no choice, Jenna," she murmured at last, her gray eyes meeting Jenna's pained brown ones. "You're our friend, and Brock's our friend. Evan and I learned long ago not to take sides, and we've never broken a promise to anyone. Brock came here a desolate man, bitter and nearly destroyed by the accident."

"What happened? Tell me!"

Martha ran her hand nervously through her short brown hair. Jenna could see the woman struggling with her thoughts, hunting for the right words.

"For pity's sake, Martha," Jenna cried, "tell me! Do you know what agony this is?"

Her eyes shimmering with tears, Martha sat down and gazed evenly at Jenna. "The day Brock left you, he was involved in a three-car accident on the way to a job in New York."

Jenna drew in a sharp breath. "My God, no! And I never heard. No one ever let me know a thing."

Her expression pensive, Martha gathered and sorted her thoughts before she spoke. "We didn't know for months ourselves. Brock disappeared for us, just as he did for you. He apparently insisted that no one be contacted but his mother and his manager, and he forbade them to leak a word. His manager succeeded in keeping it out of the papers. Brock was in a hospital in New York in critical condition for days, and he was incapacitated by a broken hip for weeks. When he could travel, he moved restlessly up and down the coast, looking for God only knows what before he finally came here."

Jenna felt an unbearable surge of guilt. She and Brock had quarreled, he had been angry, careless—

"It was just one of those things that happen," Martha murmured gently. "It wasn't because you two had split up," she added, as though reading Jenna's mind. Her words were meant to comfort, but they only confirmed Jenna's torment, for Martha had thought the same thing she had.

"How did the accident happen?" Jenna managed to ask over the pounding in her ears. These things always happened to someone else, not to the people one knew and loved.

Martha shrugged lightly. "It was raining. Somebody ran a red light. Oh, what does it matter now? Brock survived."

32

"I was so shocked to see that scar on his face," Jenna whispered. "It was almost too much to take after the surprise of seeing him so unexpectedly."

"He didn't want to stay at the house, Jenna. But he was in such turmoil, so unsettled, so hard on himself that Evan and I convinced him to see if it wouldn't help to be in a place he had considered home. He didn't feel that he belonged anywhere, what with having separated from you . . ." Her words trailed off, and Jenna's nails bit into the palms of her hands.

"How badly injured was he? I only saw the scar."

When Martha looked away, Jenna's heart plummeted. "Martha!" she implored. "Stop doing this to me."

"His hand was crushed. He'll probably never play the piano again." Reaching across the table, Martha clasped Jenna's fingers in hers. "He didn't want anyone to know what had happened to him, Jenna. He was ashamed. He didn't want pity. Evan and I promised."

Jenna bit down on her bottom lip to fight back the sudden rush of tears that blurred her vision. No, her heart and mind cried. No! Not his hand. In spite of her attempts to control her devastation at the information, a tear trickled down first one cheek, then the other. She knew what it would mean to a man like him to be injured in that way.

"Oh, Jenna, I didn't know you still cared so much," Martha moaned. "I really thought things were over for the two of you before the accident."

Jenna couldn't make her eyes meet the other woman's. "I never stopped thinking about him for a single day." Her voice was thick with the pain of a thousand regrets and heartaches as she toyed agitatedly with her coffee cup. "I went on with life, of course. What else was there to do? But to go on alone without Brock wasn't my choice."

The tears began to roll down her cheeks, and she covered her face with her hands, embarrassed because she was breaking down like this in front of her friend. The dam had broken, and

33

she was powerless to do other than sob out all the anger and frustration that had been bottled up inside her since Brock's disappearance.

Rushing over to Jenna, Martha drew her into her arms and embraced her, patting her gently on the back. "I'm so sorry," she murmured over and over again. "I'm so sorry. Evan and I did what we thought was best. We had promised him."

Martha held her, letting her cry until the sobs had subsided and she began to hiccup softly. Jenna looked at her friend sheepishly and giggled like a young girl as she wiped at her damp, tear-stained face. "Forgive me. I didn't mean to do that," she managed to say.

Martha laughed gently. "You needed to." She turned away to attend to the coffee, which was now perking loudly on the stove.

Jenna settled back down in her chair, feeling embarrassed but much better than when she had turned up on Martha's doorstep.

When Martha came back to the table to pour coffee, she gazed at Jenna as the singer brushed back wet strands of dark hair, which curled appealingly along her cheeks. "What will you do now?"

Jenna raised perfectly arched brows. There was only one thing she could do, of course. "Go back and see him. What else?"

"You're right, naturally," Martha agreed. "You have to talk to him."

"I saw a woman in the house with him," Jenna said quietly, not wanting Martha to know how that sight had upset her. She looked levelly at her friend, but her hands were wrapped tightly around her coffee cup, causing her knuckles to turn white from the pressure. "Who is she? Do you know?"

"Was she a blonde?"

Jenna nodded.

"Then it must be Dora Agate. She's Brock's physical therapist. She lives in Portland, and she comes twice a week to give him therapy. He refused to go into the city, and she volunteered to come out here."

"Is she more than his therapist?" Jenna asked bluntly, unable to be discreet in her impatience to know.

Two spots of color appeared on Martha's cheeks, and she shifted uncomfortably in her chair. "I don't know."

"You do," Jenna persisted. "Tell me, Martha."

Gray eyes met brown. "I don't know, honestly. There are rumors, but you know how rumors are."

Jenna recalled her brief glimpse of the small, sexy blonde, and even though she didn't know the woman, she instinctively sensed that Brock's therapist was at the least physically attracted to him.

A picture of Brock flashed into her mind; the scar, oddly enough, had been intriguing after she'd overcome the shock of seeing it. In some strangely fascinating way it enhanced his features, giving him a mysterious appeal that made his chiseled jaw, beautiful mouth, and startling eyes compellingly masculine instead of classically handsome, as they had been before.

Jenna realized how tense she still was when Evan walked into the room and she jumped.

"Jenna!" the tall bony man exclaimed, a big grin on his plain face. "Damn, gal! It's good to see you."

When she stood up and held her arms out to him, Evan responded by hugging her tightly to his long frame. "How are you?" he asked.

Backing away from him, Jenna found that the question brought her perilously near tears again. "To tell the truth, Evan, I'm barely hanging on. I came here to rest, and when I found Brock at the house—well, I'm not coping fantastically."

Eyeing her shrewdly, Evan shook his head. "He's had a rough go of it, Jenna. Don't be too hard on him."

Jenna opened her brown eyes wide. "Hard on him? I can't even begin to tell you how shocked I was to see him at Solace. 'Hard on *me*' might be better put, Evan. I had no idea he was here, and to see him with that scar and to hear about his hand . . ."

35

Evan nodded. "I guess it was a shock for you." He glanced at his wife, then back at Jenna. "We wanted to tell you, but—"

She held up a hand. "I know, Evan. You promised."

"That's right. And if it had been the other way around, and you had been in Brock's shoes, we would have kept our word to you."

"Yes," Jenna agreed softly. She realized that she was wrong to be angry with the Millets. They had given their word to a friend, and for them it was as simple as that. They hadn't dealt with the agony, the uncertainty, the anguish—the questions future and past which had no answers.

"Sit down, Evan," Martha said. "I'll get you some coffee."

Evan looked at his wife quizzically, and Jenna could see that he was eager to put the unpleasantness behind him. "Have we had lunch, Martha?"

The absurdity of the question broke the tension in the room, and all three of them laughed. Evan hadn't changed, Jenna told herself. The poor man still didn't know when or if he had eaten.

Laughter laced Martha's voice. "No, Evan. But the question should be whether or not you're hungry." She looked at her watch. "It's a little after noon. Why don't I heat up yesterday's clam chowder for all of us? You haven't had lunch, have you, Jenna?"

She shook her head, but she didn't know if she had enough appetite to eat a single bite. Brock was at Solace! And she didn't want him to vanish again before she had a chance to at least talk to him. Somewhere inside her a song began to play, a song that had lain buried deep within her all the long months and lonely nights Brock had been gone, a song of hope and expectation, a song that dared to come to life, and Jenna quickly squelched the forming notes.

"Where's Jud?" she asked as Martha set the table. She had been so stunned by seeing Brock that she hadn't even thought to ask about Evan's seventy-eight-year-old father, who lived with them.

36

"He's off to the far corners of the earth." Martha laughed. "You know how restless he's been since he retired? Well, one day he decided that he wanted to see some of the world before he died. I told him he had plenty of time to see it all. He's as healthy as a horse."

"And as spirited," Jenna added. She had a deep and abiding fondness for the old man, and she was glad to hear that he was well.

She stayed at the Millets' only long enough to be civil; it was good to visit with them, but her mind was on Brock thoughout the meal. What did it mean that he was here? What *could* it mean? And would he still be there when she went back? She tried to think of some way to begin a conversation with him, but suddenly it seemed impossible. Finally she had spent enough time with Evan and Martha to leave without feeling guilty, and she went back to her car.

Brock leaned back on the couch and stretched his long legs out before him. Dora had gone, and he was alone. Alone except for the thoughts which ate at him like so many hungry mouths. He hadn't known it would hurt so much to see Jenna again here in this house. When he had watched her from the doorway of the club, he had been able to remind himself that she had wanted her career above all else. She had even thought he was *jealous* of her, for God's sake. Jealous of the woman he had loved because she was succeeding. He had known then that their marriage would never work. She hadn't known him at all.

Of course he had been determined to succeed, but with everything in him he had wanted Jenna to succeed, because he loved her. He had seen the rips and the tears in the fabric of their marriage as the gap between their careers grew, and he hadn't had the heart or the guts to wait around while Jenna became more and more obsessed with her success and his failure. He hadn't had the heart, or the lack of pride, to follow in her wake and take what she would give him.

37

The marriage had been a mistake; what was the point in going on with it? But just the thought caused a deep anger to burn inside him. He had wanted to see her again, but he hadn't made any attempt to do so, other than the two phone calls and that brief moment when he had seen her in the club last night. He had told himself that if he got a bellyful of her and her success, perhaps he could go on with his own life.

Then she had come here out of the blue. He had stayed out of her life; why hadn't she stayed out of his? He hadn't wanted her to see him like this—scarred and broken. A smile twisted the cruel cut that worked its way across his upper lip.

She had been appalled by his looks, just as he had feared she would be. If he lived to be a hundred, he would never forget the way her hands had flown up to her mouth and she had recoiled at the sight of him. He traced the line of his disfigurement with his thumb. No, she wasn't here to see him; that had been apparent.

She was here for the house. She had become so successful with "Hold Love Tightly" that she could afford to live as she pleased, take all the time off she wanted when she wanted, and still be in demand when she wanted to work.

His mind strayed to that time when he had conceived the idea for "Hold Love Tightly." It had come to him in this very house, after he and Jenna had argued far into the night, then had made love until dawn. Hell, he told himself bitterly, he had no business being here, bathing himself in the past and its tormenting memories; he had been an utter fool to come.

He had started to get up off the couch to go and pack when he heard the car in the driveway. He knew that it was Jenna at the wheel, and he knew that he had to see her a final time. There were things that needed to be said—had to be said—but he felt the bitterness growing inside him as he listened to her sure steps on the walk.

Jenna automatically looked for Brock on the couch where he had been when she left. For a moment she stood just inside the living room, gazing nervously at her husband; then she sat down on the nearest chair, the one directly across from him.

"I was sorry to hear about your accident, Brock," she said stiffly, the formal tone giving no indication of how anguished she had been to learn of it. "I didn't know. No one told me."

"It doesn't matter," he said offhandedly, looking away from her.

"It does matter," she replied, more emotionally than she had intended. She had a sudden urge to touch him, to speak softly to him, to hold him to her breast. She wanted to soothe his hurts, to make things all right between them again, to make the past go away, but so much time had broadened the breach. They had both changed, she realized miserably.

She had longed to see him so often, had yearned to make him understand that she had meant nothing by her carelessly flung remarks, but now she didn't know how to tell him. They were strangers, sitting in a house they had bought together, unable to overcome a past locking them into its bitterness. Why were they starting right in with the same old self-defeating behavior?

Her voice was gentle and soothing when she spoke again. "I would have gone to you if I had only known, Brock."

His eyes flashed angrily. She *pitied* him now. He hadn't wanted her crumbs of affection then; he certainly didn't want her pity now. He lowered his gaze to stare at the hand resting on his gray pants leg, and Jenna noticed how beautifully shaped his long fingers were—the fingers of an artist, a piano player. He kept his other hand, the injured one, carefully from sight, tucked away in his pants pocket.

"I didn't mean for you to know," Brock declared firmly.

When he looked at her again, his eyes were rebellious. "I'll move out of the house within the hour. You can have it back. It was unoccupied, and I never imagined that you would come here. I know how much in demand you are."

Jenna was hurt by the sting in his words, but she drew in a steadying breath; she would not be baited by his last harsh remark. "There's no need for you to move," she said, quickly altering her plans. "I had only planned to stay a couple of weeks. I'll go back to Boston. Solace is as much yours as it is mine, and you were here first. I wouldn't have come if I had known you were here."

Their glances locked in stormy battle. "No, I suppose you wouldn't have," he muttered. "Regardless, I won't be staying."

"Don't run away again, Brock!" she flung at him. "We have to talk. You owe me that much!"

"I don't owe you a damned thing!" he retorted coldly, and Jenna's breath caught in her throat. Brock seemed almost to despise her. Was it too late for them? Had it been all along?

She licked her lips and fought down the rising panic. "I don't even know if we're divorced," she said more calmly.

A bitter smile curved his lips. "Neither do I. I would have bet my life we were."

"I didn't initiate proceedings." She tried to hold his gaze, but it was difficult.

"Neither did I. I guess that's one little piece of business you should work into your schedule."

Unable to comment, Jenna glanced out the bay window. She wanted to tell Brock that she wouldn't be the one to do it, but she remained silent. There was so much that she wanted to say, but she didn't know where or how to begin.

Her eyes traveled over him as he stood up; she could see no sign of injury in the lithe way he moved, the way he had always moved. Dressed in gray slacks that outlined his long legs and a sea-blue long-sleeved shirt which set off his aristocratic looks and compelling eyes, he was as handsome as ever—perhaps even more so with the raw sexuality of that scar.

Then she remembered what Martha had said about his hand. As though reading her mind, Brock abruptly slid it from his pants pocket and let it hang limply at his side, almost as if he were testing her reaction. Involuntarily and foolishly Jenna's gaze darted to it. She quickly looked up into Brock's eyes, aware of her mistake, but it was too late.

Those moody blue eyes had registered her appraisal and apparently misconstrued it. She wasn't appalled by his injury; she was saddened by it. But she saw that neither response would have pleased Brock. His eyes had shut out all emotion, and that once beautiful mouth had tightened into a hard, thin line. Brock was closed to her again, just as he had been in the past.

But it was different with them now; she understood that she didn't even have the right—or the nerve—to demand that he communicate with her.

The sight of his injured hand lingered in her mind, but she had enough sense not to stare at it again. There were numerous scars on it, as though Brock had had several operations, and Jenna had seen from its rigidity that he undoubtedly couldn't play the piano with it. The sight left her aching with regret; he was so very talented.

Brock's eyes held hers, but she could read nothing in the shuttered expression. "I'll move out while you're here." His gaze strayed to the window for a moment. "I can stay with the Millets for a while. Jud's away."

"I'll only be here for two weeks," Jenna said, curtailing her intended stay drastically. "*I* could stay with the Millets."

Brock shook his head firmly. "No. I'll do it."

"Why don't you keep your things here? You can soon have the house back." Jenna wanted to keep Brock at Prout's Neck, although she wasn't quite sure why; she was very much afraid that what they had had was irrevocably finished.

He looked at her, and she could only describe his appraisal as insolent. His gaze moved over her from head to toe, and she was suddenly self-conscious in the casual clothing she wore. She hadn't put on any makeup. She hadn't wanted Brock to see her like this, so unprepared, after all the time apart from him. His doubts and his indecision were now clearly apparent in his expression.

41

Seeing him here, spurning her attempts to ease the strain between them, Jenna tensed with resentment and shame. She hadn't been the only one at fault. He had been cruel to walk out on her the way he did.

He nodded, but Jenna didn't know what the gesture meant. Would he stay in the house after she had gone? Or would he vanish a second time? She was having a hard time dealing with her own confusing emotions, and she averted her eyes. When she looked back at him, she caught a brief glimpse of indescribable pain in his gaze as he studied her.

She had her pride and he had his. If he really didn't want her, she wouldn't keep trying to pick up the threads of their past. But she couldn't help but think that there was a chance he might have come back to her had he not been so badly injured. She could see how sensitive he was about his disability.

He seemed to have something he wanted to say to her, but apparently he was unwilling to say it. His facial muscles relaxed, and he murmured, "I'll go pack."

"All right," she whispered, the words lodging in her throat. She didn't want it to be this way, and she stared after him, seeing the broad shoulders she had caressed so many times in their lovemaking, the lean hips which had moved so thrillingly against hers in love's dance, the long legs which had been intertwined with her own in summer and winter, spring and fall. For thirteen months.

When he had vanished from sight, she sat numbly in the chair, wondering why she hadn't been able to tell him the thousand things on her mind. Why hadn't she asked him all the questions which had caused her to ache at night and toss and turn, cursing and trying to forget?

Was it fear of rejection? No, she told herself. She had already experienced that. It was because she was terrified that he honestly didn't love her, and she was afraid to probe too deeply lest he say so bluntly and destroy any hope she had of reestablishing some kind of rapport with him.

42

She listened to his footsteps as he made his way up the stairs; their bedroom—the bedroom, she corrected herself, for it was no longer theirs—was upstairs. She hadn't even seen it yet. She wondered bitterly if Brock had slept with that blonde here in this house; she couldn't believe that he would be so callous, but, then, she didn't know him now.

He was still her husband, but that was in name only, and perhaps even that wasn't for long. He hadn't been pleased to see her. And he had changed, she could tell that in the short time she had been with him; not in the way he related to her, that was nothing new, but in his manner, his reactions. And the change filled her with foreboding. No doubt he thought his career was over, because of his hand, and believed the future was bleak.

Jenna sat staring out the window, not knowing what else to do as she waited for Brock to leave. She didn't feel comfortable enough to start unpacking. At last his steps sounded on the stairs, and she tensed as he walked back to the living room.

"It's all yours." He tarried, and Jenna found herself praying fervently that he would offer her something for the future, something to hang on to, some hint that he still cared about her, about them. She wanted it so desperately that she almost thought she could will him to give her hope. But she was cruelly disappointed.

"I'll be going now," he said.

"Fine," she replied, knowing that it wasn't fine at all.

His eyes met hers once more, and then he was gone.

Jenna waited until he had had time enough to get out of sight, and then she went out to the car. She couldn't have sat still for another moment if her life had depended on it. She had to move, to do something; her mind was whirling and her insides were in a state of upheaval.

Taking her suitcase in one hand and some books in the other, she began unpacking the car, grateful for something to do. But even though her hands were occupied, her mind wasn't, and it went over and over the situation. She didn't know what to do,

43

what to think. Should she try to reinvolve herself in Brock's life? She couldn't bear to see him throw everything away—*their* past as well as his own. But what was she doing to herself? The eleven months away from Brock had eased some of the pain she had known. Did she want to risk starting it all over again?

As Martha had pointed out, Brock had left Jenna before his accident. Did she dare believe that had it not been for the accident, they might have gotten back together? As much as they had fought and hurt each other, she honestly believed that they had loved each other more deeply, more intensely, than most couples would in a lifetime. They were both artists, living every moment to its most glorious heights or its most agonizing depths. This had always been true of artists; sensitive, imaginative, they explored the full range of their emotions as no other people did.

She realized with a shock that she was glad she could use the accident as an excuse for her long and painful separation from Brock. Of course he had been desolate and bitter. But would he have let her see him through if they had not separated? And more important, did he care for her now at all?

CHAPTER THREE

Jenna gazed around the living room, seeing the thousand reminders of Brock: the model ships he had worked on to assuage his restlessness and driving ambition when he was tense, the seacapes of Evan's he had collected since they were in college together, and the furniture he and Jenna had spent literally weeks choosing.

Making herself stop thinking about him, she returned to the car and brought in her guitar. It was a beautiful instrument, a hand-built one Brock had had designed especially for her at a small shop in Madrid. She carried it up the steps to the music room at the end of the hall.

When she went inside, she was astonished to find Brock's baby grand piano there. Her breath locked tightly in her throat, and she walked over to the magnificent instrument and sat down on the piano stool. The keyboard cover was up, and the piano looked as if it were still being used.

Jenna ran her fingers over the ivory keys, and her mind created a picture she had seen so many times. She could visualize Brock playing, his eyes closed, his face intense with the music inside him. And she wondered if he had come to this room, this splendid room which overlooked the water, and sat in bitter misery dreaming of his shattered career, his wasted hand.

A small fire flamed inside her. Brock could still write; he had written the biggest hit on her second album. There was no reason for his career to be over. But without his piano . . . She thought of the long nights he had stayed up playing a single passage over and over on the instrument as he tried to get just what he had wanted. She couldn't imagine performing without her guitar; she had played since she was seven. Brock had played the piano since he was nine.

Dragging her fingers along the keys in sharp regret for Brock, she stood up abruptly. She knew she would be better off working now than thinking; she was too emotional to be rational. Returning to the first floor, she spent the next few hours settling in, then had a sandwich made of pastrami Brock had left in the refrigerator. She should have been tired, but she was too agitated to even consider sleep.

She roamed about the expansive house aimlessly, then gave in to the energy stalking inside her like a pacing cat. Picking up a sweater, she left the house and headed for the cliff walk. She knew the sun would soon set, and the view would be enchanting.

She was gazing out to sea, entranced by the sunset hues of purple, pink, and gold, when she came upon Brock facing the water, the wind blowing his hair into careless disarray. She stopped, riveted to the spot by the look of sheer grief written on his face. The night was cooling down rapidly as Indian summer faded into winter, and Brock looked vulnerable somehow, his tall, leanly muscled frame silhouetted as it was against the vast expanse of water and sky, his useless hand in the pocket of his gray cardigan, the other hand idly stroking his scarred cheek.

He seemed to be staring at the waves as they writhed over the dark rocks, but Jenna sensed that he was witness only to the turbulence of his own soul as he sought a way out of the pain she could read on his troubled features.

He wasn't aware that he was no longer alone, and Jenna drank in the sight of him as he stood there, his feet defiantly a little apart, a lonely figure insignificant against the pulsing ebb and flow of the waves. A gull suddenly screamed in flight overhead, and a brightly painted bell buoy responded by clanking fitfully. The sounds seemed to stir Brock from his meditations, and

Jenna sensed that he had waited until he thought no one else would be out to come to this secluded spot, but she couldn't leave him to his solitude.

"Hello, Brock," she murmured a little breathlessly.

He swung around to face her, obviously startled, and shoved his injured hand deeper into his sweater pocket. "Jenna," he said, giving her a curt nod. Then he deliberately turned back to sea, as though the woman beside him meant nothing at all.

Although Jenna was acutely disappointed, she was much too stubborn to retreat. "I'd forgotten how beautiful it is here," she said softly.

This time he turned around to gaze at her fully. His remote blue eyes studied her face, and she held her breath, waiting for him to speak, and afraid of what he would say. Finally he asked harshly, "What are you doing here, Jenna? Why have you come to Prout's Neck?"

Averting her gaze, she kicked nervously at a pebble. Then she shrugged lightly. "I don't know. Perhaps the same reason you have. Seeking solitude. A little time to myself." When she raised her eyes, she looked evenly into his, refusing to be daunted by his hostile demeanor.

"Why? Don't you have everything you want now? I hear your records on the radio all the time."

His tone was bitter and accusing. "No, I don't have everything I want," she replied. "And the lead song on one of those records you hear is yours, Brock."

He considered her response but didn't comment.

Jenna lingered only a short while longer, too tense and uncomfortable with the strained silence to stay. "I won't intrude longer on your privacy," she murmured at last, her voice edged with disappointment. Moving past him, she walked away quickly, her heartbeat sounding loudly in her ears.

"Jenna."

She spun around at the sound of her name on his lips.

"I'll walk with you."

47

Not until her breath had slipped from her lips in a ragged sigh which was absorbed by the descending night did Jenna realize that she had been holding it. "Fine," she said with a forced casualness.

Neither of them said anything, and the silence was smothering and strange in view of all that Jenna knew they should be saying. Still, Brock was by her side, and she felt that that was a beginning.

She could feel the power of him, the strength which had always emanated from him, making her aware of him as no other man ever had. She wanted to ask how he had been, *really* been, and if he truly was all right now, but she was reluctant to say anything which might drive him away. She didn't know if she knew him at all anymore, and she was feeling her way along with trembling, hesitant fingertips, lest she accidentally touch some wound still raw in his mind.

They strolled for some time along the cliff walk, their eyes on anything but each other, their minds only on each other. Jenna saw nothing of the beauty all around them.

"It's getting dark," Brock said as they worked their way around the point. "We'd better be getting back. It's turning cold."

Aware of neither the darkness nor the cold, Jenna agreed. "Yes, it's late." Her stomach was tense with anticipation; she was hoping against hope that Brock would walk her to the door of their house. This time she wasn't disappointed, and she began to talk to him cautiously, feeling a little more confident with him.

"When did you come back to Prout's Neck?" she asked, the even tone of her voice belying the turmoil she was enduring.

Did she imagine it, or did his voice roughen the slightest bit. "Two months ago."

Why here? she wanted to cry. *Because of us? Our past?* But she merely nodded. "You were here for the summer crowd, then."

"I rarely left the house."

"I see," she murmured. She couldn't resist reaching out to touch his arm. "Are you all right now, Brock?"

She flinched when he withdrew from her, as if her touch had singed his flesh. "Fine," he replied curtly.

"I'm glad," she whispered, not believing him. She suspected that he was tortured and troubled by the events of the past year. She knew before she asked that he hadn't worked professionally since his accident, but she had to make a tiny opening so that she could discuss it. "Have you worked much this year?"

Without looking at him she could feel his eyes on her, cold and resentful. "No."

She became quiet again as she felt him withdrawing further from her. She was asking all the wrong things; she had meant to keep the conversation light, but it was so hard when she wanted to know so much.

"How's your mother?" The question was asked with remarkable calm, and Jenna was pleased that she had succeeded in changing the subject so smoothly.

"She's fine. She remarried five months ago."

"How nice. I hope she's happy."

"Very."

Tense from trying to carry on the one-sided, stilted conversation, Jenna fell silent again as they approached the house. She smiled at Brock with a friendliness she was far from feeling when they walked up to the porch.

"Good night," she said, as if he were a pleasant stranger she had just met. She didn't know what else to say, how far to go, and he wasn't making it any easier for her. She wanted to beg him to open up to her, to give her a new chance and still leave her some pride.

He gazed at her in the fading light of evening as she stood before him, her heart pounding. Tentatively he reached out and let his fingers fan through her midnight hair. Then he trailed a fingertip across the sensual lines of her lower lip.

His touch stirred old memories, memories that were bitter-

49

sweet and half buried. He aroused in her a passion too long sleeping, a passion that waited only for his caress to awaken it. Jenna's lips quivered, and instinctively she kissed Brock's finger, her mouth warm and moist as she once again tasted the time of their past.

Unexpectedly Brock drew her against his hard frame with one hand, the other now exposed at his side. His arm encircled her firmly, and he groaned in tender torment as his mouth came down over hers in fiery possession.

Helpless in his embrace, a prisoner of her desire for him, Jenna molded her body to his, relishing the feel of him against her once more, the touch of her hands on his body as she traced familiar muscles outlined beneath his sweater. Her hands explored his back hungrily, and then she locked her arms around his neck, drawing him closer to her.

His mouth moved against hers almost cruelly, and she was vaguely aware of the scar which marred his beautiful upper lip. Her mouth parted under the pressure of his, and when his tongue slipped in between her teeth to explore once well known velvet territory, her tongue engaged his in a seductive dance of desire.

Jenna had dreamed of this moment a thousand times, and it was almost too much to believe that she was once again in her husband's arms. The passion she had always known with him was rekindled like dry timber caught in a wall of fire.

His lips played against hers, teasing and exploring, exciting and tantalizing. Jenna met the fire in his kiss, and her hands moved possessively down the familiar planes of his back. He stirred a hunger inside her that begged to be fed, and she could feel a reciprocal need in him as his hips pressed provocatively against hers, causing her to burn with desire for him, to yearn for that sweet oblivion in his intimate possession of her.

It didn't matter that months of bitterness and uncertainty had come between them. He was here with her now, and that was all that counted.

His lips moved against hers, sending a fever racing through

50

her blood as her tongue met his in a circling caress and his mouth worked its magic on hers. Jenna was drawn further and further into the spiraling delight inside her, fueled by Brock's heady sexuality.

His mouth left hers, and she heard him urgently whisper her name. "Jenna." His voice was so poignant and the one word so plaintive that they shattered the moment and the magic. Jenna was left feeling disappointed and deserted when Brock abruptly drew away from her.

His eyes glowed in the descending dusk, and his voice was raw with restrained passion when he spoke again. "There's no point in starting all this again. It didn't work when it began, and it won't work now."

Standing in stunned silence, Jenna could only watch as he turned away from her and strode into the night, his posture stiff, his useless hand once again imprisoned in his sweater pocket.

With trembling fingers she traced her swollen lips, lips which had so recently known such pleasure from Brock's hot, eager mouth. Fighting down a sob, she made her way into the house, her reluctant steps carrying her away from the man she still loved with a desperation bordering on obsession.

Jenna was wounded but not defeated as she shed her clothes and slipped into her bed. She tossed and turned, trying to quiet her mind so that her body could rest—a body newly awakened to passion's promise. Brock was still interested in her; his body had told her that. But was there any chance of a future with him?

Her thoughts were full of scenes from the past which reminded her of the many times she and Brock had made love in this very bed, times when Brock couldn't have turned from her. Tonight he had walked away with remarkable ease. She had been on fire for him, wanting him desperately after the interminable absence.

But, then, she had known no other man in the long months. Dan was the closest she had come to serious involvement, and she hadn't let him make love to her. A wild flame of jealousy

51

flared in the pit of her stomach. Was Brock sleeping with his therapist? Martha hadn't known, and Jenna told herself that she didn't want to know. But she did.

Why had he tormented her with his kisses if he didn't want her? Had he wanted to see if a spark of desire was still there, or had he done it only to be cruel? Her resentment grew as the mantel clock ticked off the endless minutes, counting the wasted time of Jenna's life. Restless and unhappy, she chased elusive sleep to no avail.

In desperation she eased from the bed and pulled on a silk robe, which clung provocatively to her abundant curves as she walked down the hall to the music room. The draperies were still open, and moonlight spilled across the room, irradiating Brock's piano. For a few minutes the scene held her spellbound; she was reminded of all the times she had joined Brock in this room while they both practiced their craft.

. Turning her back on the piano, she settled down on a stool, and without switching on a light she played her guitar until she was exhausted. Purged of her hurtful thoughts, she returned to her bed as the gulls began to wheel and soar against a glowing red morning sky.

Despite the turmoil Brock was creating inside her, Jenna awakened with new resolve to achieve some kind of relationship with him even if only for long enough to see what the future held. The taste of his kiss still lingered on her lips, and as she set about her morning routine, she recalled the way his body had pressed hungrily against hers. And she shivered with unsatiated desire and longing.

She hadn't slept much, but she couldn't stay in the house. She had to work off some of her anxiety. When she had drunk a cup of coffee, she dressed in gold pleated slacks and a black cashmere sweater which hugged her firm breasts. She brushed her hair until it glistened with blue-black highlights, and then she put on a touch of makeup.

Walking through the woods, she knew without consideration

52

where her path would lead; she was going to Martha and Evan's house. It was almost nine, and though she knew the Millets kept erratic hours, she suspected someone would be up. And even as she told herself that she wasn't going there to see Brock, she knew it was a lie.

The New England morning was nippy, the temperature having dipped below forty during the night, and Jenna walked briskly, enjoying the solitude. The population of Prout's Neck was small, and most of the homeowners had returned to their winter homes. A few students from the university at Portland rented houses here, but no one was about yet.

When she reached the house, Jenna knocked softly, lest Martha still be sleeping. She glanced into the front window to see if there was any sign of life, and she gazed right into Brock's penetrating blue eyes. He was standing there watching her, unmoving, and her heart began to pound alarmingly. Was he so determined to avoid her that he wouldn't even answer the door?

For a few seconds she stood there burning with humiliation; then, with false cheerfulness, she waved to him. He remained immobile, staring at her, for a little longer, and then he disappeared from view. Jenna waited tensely as she wondered if he would let her in. The seconds slipped by, and still she waited; the only sign of her frustration was her hands curled into tight fists, but she fought a terrible battle with herself to keep from leaving.

At last he opened the door. "Martha and Evan are still sleeping," he told her, his voice low, his manner indicating that he had no intention of letting her inside.

"That's too bad," she replied lightly; she brushed at the strands of black hair which moved across her face, catching in her lipstick in the slight breeze. "I wanted to invite them to dinner at the house tonight," she said impulsively. She wanted an excuse to be here, and she was determined not to let Brock's aloofness drive her away.

For a moment the two of them seemed to be suspended in time. Jenna was sure he would hear the frantic beating of her heart. The silence stretched until she thought it would break, and she expelled her breath when Brock spoke.

"Aren't you going to invite me to dinner too?" he asked, taking her by surprise. The morning light was harsh on his face, and Jenna could plainly see the scar that lashed its way across his cheek, but she saw more than that, and her woman's heart ached for him. There was an indefinable sadness in his eyes, and apparently he hadn't slept any better than she had. The dark circles told their own story, and Jenna suddenly wondered why they both didn't let go and try to rebuild their lives.

It was a tense moment for her. Of course she wouldn't rudely ignore him; he was a guest in the Millets' house. It was just that she honestly hadn't thought he would want to come to dinner. Seconds ago he had played havoc with her pride and her emotions—again. Perhaps he had been right to leave her. Perhaps she was wrong to be here at all. He needed time to let his wounds heal, and she was destroying that time for him. They hadn't been able to live together in the past; why was she still trying for the future?

But she couldn't seem to help herself. "If you have no other plans, of course you're welcome," she said, as though each word were being wrenched from her lips. Why had he even asked? Why did he keep causing such misery for them both? Why couldn't she explain the uselessness of it all to her heart and make it understand? Last night Brock had told her there was no point in starting it all again. Today . . .

Or was she reading more into his question than he had intended? Perhaps he wanted to establish some civil basis for them to begin to discuss what they must do about their legal ties.

Before he could reply, Martha suddenly appeared behind him in a blue housecoat, her thin hair a tousled mess. "Jenna. Come on in!" she exclaimed warmly. "Have some breakfast with us. I just got up."

"I hope I didn't wake you," Jenna said. "I was just telling Brock that I want to invite you to dinner this evening. I'm not going to be home most of the day, and since it's such short notice, I wanted to catch you early before you made other plans."

Martha laughed merrily. "Other plans? Like what? This isn't Boston, you know."

"Yes, I do know." Jenna wrestled with a faint smile and stepped inside when Brock finally moved so that she had room to go past him. It was so hard to appear cheerful under the circumstances.

He lingered by the door, not seeming to want to join them, but Martha wouldn't let him escape. "Come on, Brock. Let's get breakfast going." She glanced at the cup of coffee in his hand. "You haven't eaten, have you?"

"No." His gaze strayed to Jenna's glossy black hair and lovely face. "I'm not very hungry. You two go ahead."

"Nonsense!" she cried. "I won't have a guest in my house who won't eat with me. Now, come on back to the kitchen with us."

Her imperious manner caused Brock to laugh, and Jenna thrilled to the husky sound; she hadn't heard his laughter in so long. With Martha, Brock seemed much his old self, and Jenna envied Martha the easy rapport she had with him. "You sure have a way with men, Martha," he teased. "A drill sergeant couldn't be more effective."

The confident Martha laughed with him. "Whatever works," she retorted, tying her sash more tightly around her waist and tossing back her disheveled hair as she went into the kitchen.

"Get yourself some coffee, Jenna," she said. "Brock's apparently made a fresh pot. Mmm, it smells delicious, doesn't it?"

Brock came into the room, and Jenna found it necessary to walk around him to go to the coffeepot. She was intensely conscious of him this morning, the masculine vitality that was part of his very essence. She longed to wrap her arms around him and give him a good morning kiss as she had done so many times before, but she offered him a tentative smile instead. He didn't return it, but she could feel him watching her as she poured her coffee, and it was all she could do to keep her hands steady. The

55

air fairly crackled with tension, but everyone pretended not to notice.

While Martha cooked, Brock casually leaned against the counter. Jenna, sitting at the table, directed most of her attention to Martha, as did Brock, but she was acutely aware of her husband as he lounged before her, clad in blue jeans and a pale blue sweater, looking every inch the appealing male. He made an attempt to hide his scarred hand, and Jenna was careful not to look at it.

Soon the smell of bacon cooking permeated the room, and Jenna began to relax a little. The atmosphere in Martha and Evan's home had always been conducive to relaxation, but the fact that Brock was here, grudgingly sharing this time with her, diminished Jenna's usual pleasure.

The tantalizing aroma of coffee and bacon soon brought a sleepy Evan stumbling from the bedroom, his hair in wild disarray, a grin on his plain face.

"Morning," he mumbled, stifling a yawn. "Jenna. Brock." He nodded in their direction, then dropped down into a chair across from Jenna. "Boy, am I bushed," he groaned, smoothing down his hair with both hands. "I painted until two A.M."

"You can eat and go back to bed," Martha said soothingly as she carried a steaming cup of coffee over to the table. "Jenna's invited us to dinner this evening."

Evan smiled, and his sunny smile transformed his face. "That's a great idea. Remember how much fun we used to have?" He shut up abruptly, his face turning a rosy pink as he looked guiltily at first Brock, then Jenna.

"Yes," Jenna agreed, wanting to make Evan feel comfortable. "Those were marvelous times, weren't they?"

Evan nodded, but he didn't reply. Brock toyed with his coffee cup for a minute, then lifted it to his lips and drained it. He didn't comment at all.

"This evening will be wonderful too," Martha said, cracking eggs into the bacon grease and putting toast in the toaster. It was clear that even she didn't believe her words, but she was working hard at trying to be cheerful, despite the disquieting atmosphere.

"Is there something I can do to help with breakfast?" Jenna asked.

"Yes. Pour the orange juice, if you will."

Walking over to the refrigerator, Jenna self-consciously smoothed down her black sweater, then opened the refrigerator door and reached for the juice. She felt ridiculously like a young girl trying to behave normally in front of a reluctant suitor, and she resented Brock for putting her in this position. He watched her boldly, either not caring about or not noticing the looks that passed between Martha and Evan while he stared at Jenna.

Any other time she would have asked if each of them wanted juice, but this morning she set about the business of pouring it into four glasses, grateful for something to do. Brock hadn't said he would come to dinner, and Jenna told herself it would be best if he didn't; all of them were uncomfortable, and she didn't want to endure an evening like this morning. Still, she felt that she had had no choice but to invite him. She sighed. She admitted to herself that she wanted him to come, for she couldn't forget him until she knew that she had no other alternative.

In view of his attitude her desire to rekindle what they had known seemed a hopeless one. Brock was too bitter, too hostile. There seemed no point in subjecting herself to more misery, and yet as long as a spark remained between them, she felt that she had to try once more.

Breakfast was soon served, and Jenna and Martha sat down, leaving the chair between them vacant. Strolling over, Brock seated himself. Jenna was unable to help noticing the way he held his injured hand in his lap, as if he didn't want anyone to see it, but she wasn't fool enough to let Brock catch her observing him.

Amazingly Martha soon had the conversation rolling smoothly—if only superficially—and even Brock seemed to be enjoying the meal. Foolishly Jenna began to relax.

When the meal was over, Brock left with Evan to see the

57

painting Evan had worked on so late. Martha automatically began to clear the table and wash dishes, and Jenna picked up a dishtowel so that she could dry.

"You do realize that Brock has changed, don't you, Jenna?" Martha asked with a casualness that veiled deep concern.

Jenna could feel her heart beat more rapidly. Was it so obvious that she still wanted him? Was that why Martha felt the need to say this?

She shrugged lightly. "Yes, and not for the better."

"Oh, I don't know that it isn't for the better in some ways. In others he's become a shell of his former self, bitter, resentful, mistrusting. He's in the process or reassessing himself and his values. But no one can recapture the past, certainly not Brock, now that he will never play again."

"How do you see him as changing for the better?" Jenna asked, not able to see it for herself.

"He isn't as driven now. He's learning to live with himself, to look at himself and others more realistically."

"I hadn't noticed," Jenna replied honestly. She looked into Martha's gray eyes. "Does he talk about me, Martha? Do you think he still cares?"

Jenna felt crushed when Martha looked away. "He asked if I thought you would come back to the house when he first arrived. After that he never again mentioned you." She pretended to be engrossed in the pan she was washing. "You still love him very much, don't you?"

Jenna was suddenly shy about admitting her weakness for Brock; after all, he had left her, humiliating her terribly. "I'm not sure. I want to find out."

"Do you really?" Martha asked, her voice guarded. "Sometimes it's best to put the past behind us and go on." Her gray eyes met Jenna's velvet brown ones. "I don't think Brock will ever again be the man you knew, Jenna. I don't know if he'll ever be happy now. I don't need to tell you that music was his life. He's got a long uphill battle before him."

Jenna shook her head. "No, you don't need to tell me." A smile trembled on her lips. "But his life's not over, for heaven's sake. These things happen to lots of people. He's fortunate in that he can still compose."

"And what if it happened to you? What if you could never again play your guitar professionally?"

"I don't know," Jenna murmured softly, disappointed that Martha was adding to her confusion and uncertainty. "I've thought about it. At least I could still sing, just as Brock can compose, but it's like losing half of you."

"He's crazy about it!" Evan exclaimed, bursting back into the room. "He loves my painting."

Jenna marveled at the artist's insecurity. Evan never knew if his work was good until someone praised it—and someone always did. He sold almost every painting he painted, and his work hung in galleries and museums all over the world. Inspired by his idol, Winslow Homer, Evan had moved to Prout's Neck from Kentucky, and he had achieved phenomenal success, almost as if he had absorbed some of the Homer magic by walking the same ground, living in the same area, studying the same sea Homer had studied.

"Of course he loved it," she said. "You're a great painter, Evan. Don't you know that by now?"

He grinned sheepishly. "I think every one I paint may be my last good piece. Isn't insecurity hell?"

"Yes, it is," she agreed sincerely. "I'd like to see the painting. You showed it to Brock," she added.

She knew before she asked that Evan wouldn't let her see it. He and Brock had been like brothers since college; they shared the good and the bad, but Evan didn't even let Martha see his work until it was completed. It never seemed to bother Martha, but it had always made Jenna feel a bit left out, though she understood his reluctance.

"Come on, Jenna," he said. "I can't do that. But I'll show it to you as soon as I've finished."

Her gaze shifted to Brock. He stood beside Evan with his arms folded, his bad hand hidden, and Jenna wondered if he kept it hidden only from her.

"It's magnificent, as always," Brock said. However, he was talking more to Evan than to Jenna.

After she had stayed only a short while longer, Jenna excused herself to go to Portland. Her mind was filled with thoughts about Brock as she walked back to her house.

What would he do with his life now? Did he hope and dream that one day his hand would be well and he could play the piano again? She couldn't imagine Brock living on dreams; he had always been so decisive, so certain of what he wanted to do with his life—and so determined to do it. But Martha had said he had changed in the way he viewed himself and others. Did that include his wife?

When she had gone into her house, she went upstairs to the bathroom to freshen her makeup, and as she stood gazing at the tall, dark-haired woman before her, she knew that, just as Brock had changed, so had she. Her career was at its height, but her personal life was a disaster. Oh, there were plenty of men who were interested in her, she knew, but Brock hung stubbornly in her mind, tormenting her, evoking memories that she couldn't forget, refusing to let her go.

Dabbing fresh lipstick on her full mouth, she decided not to keep mulling over painful facts; she would take one day at a time and see what happened. That was all she could do.

CHAPTER FOUR

It was late afternoon when she returned from Portland. Even though she and Brock both had kept clothing and odds and ends at Solace, Jenna had purchased a new dress for the evening. She needed the kind of lift a new dress could give, and, she confessed to herself, she wanted to look special just in case Brock did come to dinner.

After she had taken the bags from the car, she went to the kitchen and started the New England boiled dinner, leaving corned beef to simmer for two and a half hours while she dressed.

She soaked in the tub for an hour, then slipped into a silk robe and smoothed rose-scented lotion on her hands and legs. She was startled when she heard the peal of the doorbell; her guests weren't supposed to arrive until much later. Seven o'clock. She couldn't imagine who would be at the door, unless it was someone calling for Brock. Barefoot, she hurried down the stairs.

When she pulled the door open, she was surprised to see her husband standing on the porch. She blinked twice, and a betrayingly nervous hand strayed to her hair, tied up on her head with a red ribbon. Her face was flushed from the bath and she didn't have on a bit of makeup. Was that amusement she saw flicker briefly in Brock's eyes, or disdain? It had disappeared so quickly that she couldn't tell.

"You forgot to tell Martha what time you intend to have dinner."

Jenna knew a moment of agitation. Did that mean that Brock

was coming? "Did I?" she asked, honestly unable to remember. She had thought she had said, but she had been so flustered by Brock that perhaps she hadn't.

"It's—it's at seven o'clock."

"Thanks." His gaze traveled over her, and then he turned on his heel to go.

"Brock!"

He glanced back over his shoulder carelessly. "Would you like to come in?" Jenna was holding her breath, awaiting his answer anxiously.

"No, thanks." He turned away from her again, and she watched as he moved down the long walk and stepped onto the sidewalk.

Jenna waited until he was out of sight, and then she kicked the door shut with her foot. "Damn!" she exploded, angry with him and herself. Why had he been the one to come, anyway? Why hadn't Martha or Evan come? Brock hadn't even accepted her invitation.

Storming back up the steps, she went to her room and dragged her new dress from its bag, then tossed it on the bed. Why was she concerned about how she looked, anyway? Maybe Brock wouldn't show up, and if he did, what would it amount to?

She took several deep breaths, trying to calm down, but it wasn't until she had done her hair and face that she stopped fuming. She did love the dress she had selected; the color was cherry-red, her favorite, and it was a tantalizing bit of at-home wear with its thigh-high slits on each side.

Pulling the garment over her head, Jenna smoothed it into place. She wore it without a bra, and it clung to her high, rounded breasts as if it had been made for her. This was the kind of dress she had known would get a whistle from Brock two years ago. But now . . .

She left her hair long, a midnight vision shimmering about her shoulders. By the time she had slipped her backless red heels on, she was feeling better; she vowed to have a good time this evening, regardless of what happened.

When she returned to the kitchen, it was time to cook the vegetables, and she set about the chore with a vengeance. But she couldn't stop the flood of thoughts about Brock.

Preparing the hors d'oeuvres, setting the table, chilling the wine, and getting out the tall candles, Jenna managed to while away the next hour. Finally it was time for her guests, and she awaited them in nervous anticipation, terrified that Brock wouldn't come—and terrified that he would.

The doorbell rang precisely at seven, and Jenna put on a bright smile; she vowed to show no reaction, no matter who appeared. She opened the door to find all three of them there, and she smiled more beautifully. "Come in."

"You look gorgeous!" Martha cried upon entering the house. "I love that gown. Girl, you've really come up in the world."

Jenna laughed lightly, pleased by the attention in Brock's presence. Her eyes darted in his direction, and she saw that he was appraising her intently, his eyes scanning her flushed face and long hair, then her shapely figure in the clinging red dress. A hint of long, lovely leg showed from the slits, and Jenna saw Brock's thick blond brows arch almost imperceptibly at the view.

"Doesn't she look beautiful, fellows?" Martha asked, turning to the two men when they were all inside.

Evan grinned. "She always did look good to me, no matter what she wore."

Giving him a playful slap, Martha joked, "Watch it, buddy."

Jenna thanked Evan for his compliment, but it was Brock's approval she had really sought, and she didn't get it. At least not verbally. He still hadn't stopped looking at her, and she began to grow uneasy under his penetrating appraisal. Did he despise her now? Did he see what she was doing, just as Martha had? She pressed her lips together nervously; at least he had come.

When Jenna had asked them to be seated in the living room,

she went to the kitchen to get the wine and snacks. She gasped when someone came up behind her, and she whirled around to find Brock standing there.

"Nervous?" he asked softly, his eyes holding hers with a hypnotic gaze. Jenna almost hated him for the perceptive question.

"No, of course not. I've been under a lot of stress lately," she said defensively.

"I came to help you with the hors d'oeuvres," he said after an unnerving pause, and Jenna shoved a plate of stuffed celery at him.

She was surprised to see him instinctively reach for it with both hands, and her lips parted in anguish when she saw that he couldn't even grasp with his left hand. A spasm of pain altered his facial features only momentarily. Jenna saw stiff fingers clutch helplessly without holding, and she saw the pain written on Brock's face change to fury, again only briefly. Then he skillfully balanced the plate on one hand, pivoted, and disappeared into the living room.

So shaken was she by the experience that Jenna turned around and clutched the counter for support. God knew she wouldn't have done that to him for anything. She could feel his humiliation and rage at being unable to do so simple a chore as carry a dish.

She didn't know that Brock had already come back to the kitchen, determined to show her that he was no less a man than he had once been. His jaw muscles twitched ominously when he saw her leaning against the counter, and he didn't know whether to go or stay.

He had been an imbecile to come here and risk another confrontation. The kiss had proven to him that he couldn't be around her without wanting her; but he had made his choice long ago, and now there was no turning back. Not the way he was. The accident had robbed him of the chance to find out if they could get back together, and it had irrevocably erased any possibility of a future for them on any terms. He could see that now.

He moved forward, making sure that Jenna could hear his steps on the tile, and she was surprised and deeply disturbed to see that he was back when she glanced over her shoulder. She quickly moved away from the counter, but she was afraid that he had already seen her supporting herself against it.

"What else?" he demanded curtly, the anger flickering in his eyes.

• Jenna bit down painfully on her lip; surely he didn't think she had embarrassed him on purpose. She looked around wildly for something he could carry with one hand, but before she could give him anything, he reached for the platter with the shrimp on it, apparently meaning to show her that he could manage it.

"That'll be fine," she said thickly.

When he had gone again, she took several deep breaths, then picked up the wine and a couple of glasses. She hurried toward the living room, not wanting Brock to catch her in the kitchen again.

He had just set the shrimp platter down when she entered the room. "We need two more glasses, and that's it," she told him, her voice unusually husky with chagrin.

Nodding, he brushed past her, and Jenna tensed as the warmth of his body touched hers. Martha looked at her curiously when she walked over to the coffee table to set the wine and glasses down, but mercifully she merely asked, "Can I help with anything?"

"No, thanks. Brock and I have it under control." Jenna couldn't look at the other woman, so upset was she by her encounter with her husband. It was unsettling to have him help with guests as he had done countless other times, as if nothing were wrong, as if they were not slowly destroying each other.

Going over to the stereo unit, she put on some mood music, then settled down tensely in a favorite rocking chair, glad for the soothing motion as she moved back and forth, trying to dissipate some of her distress.

Brock sat down on the couch with Evan and Martha, and once

again Martha was the leader in the conversation. She had a knack for making easy chitchat, and Jenna was grateful to soon find the four of them discussing which songs they liked best on the charts.

"I'm dying to hear you sing your new one," Martha told Jenna. "I've heard it on the radio dozens of times now, but there's nothing like the real thing."

Jenna glanced uncomfortably at Brock; she had just seen that he couldn't hold a plate with his hand, and she didn't want him to be further reminded that he could no longer play either.

She smiled evasively at Martha. "I would only disappoint you. You're spoiled from hearing the record. The real thing often isn't nearly as good. That background music helps tremendously, as I'm sure you know."

Martha laughed lightly. "Don't be modest. We all know you're terrific, and I insist on hearing you play after dinner. We all want to hear you."

Jenna was surprised by Martha's request; she was sure the woman was sensitive to Brock, and she could only conclude that Martha thought it would serve some purpose—though at the moment Jenna couldn't see what. She was relieved when Evan spoke.

"Remember how dreadful I was our first Christmas together? I had had too much to drink and insisted on doing a duet with you."

Jenna couldn't restrain her laughter, and even Brock smiled. Evan *had* been incredibly bad; the poor man couldn't sing a note, and he had been all the funnier because he had been inordinately pleased with himself. In a playful mood Martha had recorded the song on the tape deck built into Jenna's stereo unit, and Evan had refused to believe it was he on the tape for two solid weeks. Finally Martha had coaxed him into singing again, and then he had no longer been able to deny it.

"Dinner's ready," Jenna announced while the mood was still light.

Once again Evan and Martha chose their chairs so that Brock was left to sit next to Jenna. She lit the candles and turned off the lights as soon as she had placed all the dishes on the table.

Martha giggled sweetly. "Oh, Evan," she cooed, "isn't this romantic? Why don't we ever do this at home?"

In the candlelight Jenna could see Evan blush, and she and Brock both laughed. Their eyes locked briefly, and Jenna's breath caught in her throat. The soft light gentled Brock's disfigurement, and he was so appealingly handsome that she ached for him in that moment when their gazes touched. She was the one to look away, afraid that he would see how much she still cared.

Brock took a bite of the meat which had been passed to him. "This is delicious," he told her as casually as if he were talking with a stranger.

She didn't hear any sharpness in his words, and she murmured, "Thank you." She had cooked the New England dinner because she knew that it had once been Brock's favorite. She also had apple cobbler with whipped cream for dessert; that, too, had once been something he loved.

The meal passed in reasonable pleasantness. After cobbler and coffee the foursome again went to the living room. Although Jenna had the heat turned on, Evan insisted upon making a fire in the massive fireplace. After several false starts he finally succeeded, and the flames came to life, bright and golden with their promise of warmth and dancing light.

"Go get your guitar," Martha insisted, and Jenna was sorry she was asking again. She had hoped that the subject was closed. There was no need to remind Brock of his misfortune.

"I don't think so. Not tonight," Jenna said.

"Why not?" Martha persisted.

Jenna was surprised by her friend's insistence. She frowned at the woman, but to no avail. "Come on, Jenna. We'd all love to hear you."

After giving Brock an uncomfortable glance Jenna firmly

shook her head. "I'm really not in the mood tonight, Martha." And that was an incredible understatement, she could have added.

Her gaze locked with Brock's again. "I want to hear you sing 'Hold Love Tightly,' " he drawled unexpectedly, his blue eyes enigmatic.

Jenna fidgeted nervously. Why? Why was he doing this to her? She didn't want to sing, and especially not that song. Brock had given it to her as a gift on her birthday, after one of their stormy quarrels and reconciliations. It was so personal, and though she had been driven to record it, maybe in an attempt to purge herself of him or perhaps subconsciously in the hope that he would hear it, she had never imagined playing it for him. It would disturb her too much. As he continued to gaze at her in silence, she found herself wondering if he knew what a success his song was, or how eager other artists were for something he had written.

"You're all very flattering," she murmured, looking desperately for a way to change the subject, "but I don't think I'm up to singing tonight. I came here to rest, you know. Why don't we . . ."

Brock didn't wait for her to finish. "I'd consider it a favor if you sang the song, Jenna."

Her words died in her throat at Brock's solemn request. Without comment she rose stiffly, her chin held high, and walked out. When she came back, she settled down on a bearskin rug in front of the fireplace and bent over, the guitar resting on her lap. Her dark hair tumbled toward her face, and the flickering flames from the pine logs cast soft gold over her skin and shining hair. The lovely red dress fell away from her thighs, and she was unaware of how beautiful she was in the firelight.

She was as nervous as she could ever remember being, and her fingers shook as she strummed the strings of the guitar. She had played for the three of them so many times before, but now it was different. She didn't know if she could get through the song, but she knew for some reason she couldn't explain even to herself that she had to try.

She cleared her throat, then swallowed hard, stalling for time. God, this was awful. She was terrified that she would break down, but she bravely began to sing the words, her voice more husky than usual. This time she wasn't able to lose herself in the music, and she could sense the tension building stronger and stronger as the beautiful notes filled the waiting stillness.

Across from her Brock sat rigidly in grave silence, watching her perform the song he had written for her. He had never heard her sing it, not even when he had given it to her, and now he cursed himself for asking her. She was so bewitching; he had almost made himself forget how much she moved him when she sang, her face transformed by her music, her voice husky and vibrant. But now he recalled all too easily how he succumbed to her spell. He closed his eyes briefly as desire washed over him—desire and an agonizing regret at the loss of what they had once had together. In retrospect their relationship seemed so fragile and wondrous, a love that should have been nurtured like a delicate flower until it was strong enough to survive the stress of grueling schedules and professional insecurities.

The words of his song seemed to mock him as the voice of the woman he loved enveloped him, tormentingly and hauntingly reminding him that if he didn't hold love tightly, it would soon slip away. Had he had a premonition that the love they had known could never survive? The words beat at his thin threads of self-control, and he didn't know if he could endure it until the bittersweet message gave its last warning.

His mind trembled under the weight of a thousand memories, and his soul twisted in despair as Jenna's provocative voice caused him to remember what he had tried so hard to forget.

After the accident he had called her name for days—but only in his heart. He had known that he couldn't ask her to come to him. He had left her, just picked up and vanished, because he hadn't wanted to trail in her wake as her career soared higher and higher. He couldn't return to her a broken man; a confused, embittered man who was faced with the task of rebuilding a shattered life. He knew now that it was over. And he was only punishing himself by being here. He realized that he had come to see if he could be with her and not long to draw her into his arms, hold her to his heart, love her. And he had found out.

Jenna's voice cracked, and Brock gazed at her, his lids narrowed so that no one would see what a fool he was. Her eyes met his, and she faltered but recovered with the practice of a true professional. She thought that she would die before she finally sang the last words of the song. She had never suffered anything so painful in her entire life; the words seemed to deride her, for it was much too late to hold love tightly. Love had spurned her, and she realized now that it was useless to go on dreaming that Brock cared. He couldn't have asked her to sing this song if he did.

A thousand distressing possibilities went through her mind, and she wondered if Brock wasn't purposely tormenting her. Was he sorry that he had written the song for her? Did he despise her for having recorded it? He didn't know, of course, why she had done it, and maybe he never would.

At last she made it to the end, and she thrust the guitar from herself, turning to the fire to toss more wood on it so that her audience wouldn't see the sheen of the tears brightening her eyes. No one said a word; Martha's tongue, too, had been silenced for once, and it was agony for Jenna to face any of them.

"I told you it would be disappointing," she said, making herself turn back around, but she couldn't inject any levity into her voice, as she had meant to do.

"It was stunning," Martha said solemnly. "I was so moved, Jenna." She stared pensively at Brock for a moment, then looked down at her watch. "Good heavens! Is it nine already? We've got to go."

Jenna gazed at her friend. "Go? Now?"

"Jud's phoning later. In his last letter he mentioned he'd call

tonight, and he'll be upset if we're not there to talk to him."
Martha made a wry face, and Jenna realized that the woman's
intention was to leave Jenna alone with Brock. The idea un-
nerved her; she couldn't imagine anything more harrowing at the
moment. "Can't you stay a little longer?" she implored.

"No, really we can't." Martha turned back to Brock, confirm-
ing Jenna's suspicions. "You don't need to come with us, of
course. You have a key. Come home when you're ready."

As the Millets stood up so did Brock. Jenna rose, too, and
propped her guitar against the wall. She wanted them all to go
and leave her alone with her misery. She couldn't stay in Prout's
Neck now. She would go back to Boston, where she belonged.
She was infinitely sorry she had taken up Brock's challenge and
sung. She had quite nearly been broken completely by it.

"Tell you what," Martha said as she and Evan walked out
onto the porch. "You come to our place tomorrow night. I'll
make some pretzels, we'll have lots of beer on hand, and we'll
play cards all evening."

"Thanks, Martha." Jenna would have agreed to anything just
to get them to leave.

Both Martha and Evan thanked her for the evening, then
faded into the night. To Jenna's consternation Brock lingered
behind, gazing at her as she stood uncertainly, waiting to shut
the door. The night was cold, but she felt only the numbness in
her heart.

Only moments ago Brock had warned himself of the futility
of the situation with Jenna, but now, knowing he should leave
as had Martha and Evan, he found that he couldn't until—until
—he didn't know what. It was as if she had touched him with
her very own magic, and he couldn't go away until she willed it.
He stood before her in awkward silence, wanting to go and
wanting to stay.

"Isn't there some wine left?" he drawled at last.

Jenna couldn't believe she was hearing him correctly. Surely
he didn't want to stay and punish her further. She was barely

coping now. She glanced out into the darkness, but Martha and Evan were already gone.

"Jenna?"

"Yes," she murmured.

"Is there wine left?"

She nodded. Why was he going on with this? Why didn't he leave?

"You don't want to waste it, do you?"

He had asked that same question the first night she had cooked dinner for him, the first night they had made love. "No," she whispered, wondering why. Then she stepped inside and waited for him to follow. When she closed the door, her hand was shaking.

Brock sat down on the couch and picked up his wineglass. Jenna refilled it, her hand quivering slightly. Brock studied her from beneath furrowed brows, but he didn't speak.

Nervous, Jenna sat back down cross-legged on the rug and glanced at Brock, but he wasn't looking at her; his gaze was resting on the wine in his glass. He swirled the dark liquid around, and Jenna could see that his own emotions were spinning in a whirlpool as dark as the wine. She watched as he finally tilted the glass to swallow its contents, and she knew that he had made more than that simple decision when he did so. She looked away and studied the colorful fire as it played low on the partly burned logs.

"You sing more beautifully than ever."

She looked up shyly, no longer certain of her appeal to him. "I wasn't very good tonight."

Their gazes held. "I thought you were."

Uneasy, she averted her eyes, searching for something to say. "Have you written any songs recently, Brock?"

A slow smile spread over his sensual lips. "Yes, in fact I have." Unexpectedly he moved forward, leaving the couch to kneel before her. Reaching out, he cupped her chin in his hand. "Another one for you, Jenna."

She didn't know if he was mocking her or not, but she gathered her courage to ask him to tell her more, taking heart that he was writing. It was good to know that he had been working, regardless of the reason. "What's the title?"

" 'When Love Is Gone.' "

Jenna blanched. Had he written the song for her to sing, or did he mean the message was for her? She didn't dare ask, for she was sure she already knew the answer. She was glad he was writing, she reminded herself, but that didn't ease the heartache. She didn't need to hear the song to imagine what the words would be.

She didn't know what to say, and for a few seconds only the murmurings of the fire could be heard, talking quietly as if its earlier crackling chatter had been hushed by Brock's song title. She made herself look into his eyes, and she was hurt by the anguish she saw there.

"What happened to us, Jenna?" he asked in such a troubled voice that she felt a sob rise in her throat. Her lips quivered uncontrollably, and Brock reached out to still the trembling with his fingertip. Jenna stifled a sigh, and she wondered if the agony would ever go away. Brock traced her full lower lip with his finger, trailing it sensuously around the outline.

Catching his finger between her lips, Jenna kissed it, her warm, moist lips clinging gently. As Brock lowered his head he groaned softly, and though Jenna sensed his reluctance to give in to the moment, his mouth closed down possessively over hers.

She could taste the anger in his kiss, but there was something more too. Longing? Regret? Love? Or was it only desire? She couldn't tell, and at the moment she didn't care. His lips moved hungrily against hers, burning and demanding; then suddenly his mouth became intensely gentle. Jenna held her breath, afraid this moment would never come again.

When Brock's fingers wove their way into her long hair and he eased Jenna down on the softness of the bearskin, she released her breath in a ragged moan. He held her tightly to him as if he

73

feared she might run away, and Jenna wrapped her arms around his neck, glorying in the feel of his muscled body.

At last his mouth freed hers, and her breath came more rapidly as his lips moved over her eyes and face urgently, tasting the clean sweetness of her skin. His lips returned to her mouth as though he couldn't get enough of it; and he placed teasing love bites all along her lower lip, his breath warm and sweet on her skin.

When he traced the outline of her lips with his tongue, Jenna's tongue touched his, and once again they kissed, savoring the joy too long missing. Brock's tongue stole into her mouth, traced her teeth, then retreated. Jenna's followed into the warmth of his mouth, and she began to yearn for the fulfillment of his loving. In that single pulsing moment it was as if the past did not exist. Here and now it seemed that they had never experienced such devastating blows to their marriage.

Brock's lips left hers to scatter hot kisses along her throat and down to her rapidly rising and falling bosom. His tongue sought a nipple to tease it through the material of her dress, making the peak stand taut and aching beneath the pressure of his circling caresses. As his mouth closed down over the throbbing tip Jenna whispered, "Brock, oh, Brock, it's been so long."

Her voice seemed to trigger something inside him. "Too long," he returned huskily. "Too damned long." Then he moved away from her and stood up.

Jenna lay where he had left her on the thick plushness of the rug, and she experienced an emotion remarkably near panic as she watched him walk toward the door.

There was a loud snap when he flipped off the wall light switch, and Jenna's breath rushed out in relief as he came back toward her, the glow of the fire causing his shadow to loom large on the wall.

This time he knelt down to gaze at her in the wavering light of the fire. Jenna lay before him, willing him to want her, to love her. Brock trailed both hands down her face, exploring her features, tracing them almost reverently as if he wanted to remember them forever. Bending over her, he kissed her lips lingeringly; her mouth was warm and clinging. Then Brock shook his head.

"Oh, Jenna, Jenna," he murmured in torment. He closed his eyes for an instant, and his face grew taut with hopelessness. "No," he groaned.

In one swift movement he rose and left her. Jenna watched in disbelief as he slipped from the room's darkness and into the deep night. The door shut behind him with a finality that was shattering. Jenna curled up into a tight ball and wished she could die.

CHAPTER FIVE

Angry with himself, Brock shoved his hands into his pockets and made his way through the darkness toward the cliff walk. He had been a fool to think that he could spend time with Jenna and not desire her. She was a living flame burning in his soul.

He had been a bigger fool to think that he could hold her and recapture what they had once had. No one could go back. Least of all a man whose life had been altered as his had.

But he had been the biggest fool of all when he had almost made love to her, because one more time in her arms was never enough—and always too much.

His frustration was so great that he freed his hands from his pockets and repeatedly hit the injured one against the other until spasms of pain ricocheted up his arm. His seething anger momentarily forgotten as the pain registered, Brock swore bitterly, then continued down to the water's edge. He shoved the mute reminder of his misery back into his pocket as he stood staring at the wicked darkness of the water. As restless and churning as his own emotions, it spewed and crashed against the black rocks in the pale glow of a haunting, faraway moon.

A painful and disquieting realization dawned on Brock as he kept his lonely vigil by the water's edge: he suddenly knew why he had come back to Prout's Neck. The chains that had dragged him here were his memories of Jenna. Jenna smiling as she frolicked on the beach in a skimpy bikini, Jenna lying like a goddess on the sandy shores, Jenna laughingly luring him into the shower to help her wash away the sand, Jenna pressing her magnificent body against his, Jenna heating his blood in the darkness of their bedroom, far away from the hustle and heart of Boston, where she was a star.

The sea seemed to mock him as it sent waves pounding against the shore, thundering a single word—Jenna—then dragging that word, and Brock's heart, back to sea.

A lone gull cried out its misery to the dark night, and Brock wondered if it, too, had lost its mate. He had promised himself that he wouldn't love Jenna anymore, that she was in the past, but the heart didn't listen to promises. He loved her as much as ever; he wanted her as his wife again. And where did he go from here?

Jenna was startled from her restless sleep by the insistent ringing of a bell. Disoriented, she groped along the night table for the telephone, then became aware of her surroundings. She slipped out from under the covers, threw on a robe, then stumbled down the stairs, smoothing the robe over her hips enroute. When she opened the door to see Dan and her mother, she mustered a weak smile.

"Good morning."

"Good morning, Jenna," Joan O'Neil said. "I hope you don't mind us coming. It was my idea. Your manager has been phoning repeatedly, and I needed to get in touch with you. Besides," she added, "I wanted to see you." They both knew she could have called Evan and Martha.

Shaking her head wearily, Jenna opened the door wider. "Of course I don't mind, Mother, but you could have saved yourself the trip by calling." Her eyes skimmed down the slim figure, and a surge of love went through her as she assessed the plain brown dress. Joan O'Neil could be a very good-looking woman if she only took the effort, Jenna reminded herself for the hundredth time, but apparently Joan had lost the will to love again when Jenna's father died.

77

Jenna's eyes strayed to Dan, who stood beside Joan, looking sheepish. "You two look like children who've been caught with their hands in the cookie jar. Come on in. It's cold out."

"How are you, Jenna?" Dan asked anxiously.

She leaned forward to receive his kiss on her cheek. "I'm all right. How are you?"

"Fine, now that I see you."

"I'm sure I don't look that good," she teased, leading them into the living room.

"You obviously aren't dying of loneliness," Dan remarked. "Looks like you had a party."

Jenna laughed gently. "The Millets," she said with a shrug, but she couldn't meet her mother's eyes. She could still feel the way Brock had touched her so enticingly, so tantalizingly, just hours ago, and she was both embarrassed and pained by the memory of the way he had left her.

She stared at the living room, seeing it as her guests must see it—the platters with dried hors d'oeuvres, the empty wine-glasses, the ashes of last night's fire. As her eyes skimmed over the bearskin rug which had cradled her body when Brock caressed her she quickly turned away.

"Have you had breakfast?"

Dan nodded. "We ate on the way up."

"Good." Running her hands across her face wearily, Jenna murmured, "I was asleep when you rang the bell. Will you make yourselves at home for just a few minutes while I take a quick shower and get dressed?"

Her mother's curious brown eyes appraised Jenna. "You go right ahead. Dan and I know our way around the place."

Jenna slipped back into the hall and up the stairs. As she entered the bedroom she drew a resigned breath. She told herself that she was glad Joan and Dan had come, for they were a much-needed distraction, and they would keep her from fleeing back to Boston like a frightened rabbit. She had been singed once again by Brock's fire, and she was afraid of the blaze now.

She had realized all too plainly when he left her last night that there was no hope for them. He would never believe that she loved him. Martha was right; he had changed—too much. Her career and his had always been a major source of conflict; now they were an insurmountable obstacle. She very much wished that she hadn't accepted "Hold Love Tightly" as a gift; in fact, she wanted Brock to have the money the record earned. But she didn't dare offer it to him; she was sure his pride would be hurt.

A warm shower revitalized Jenna somewhat and did its best to soothe her troubled mind. When she had dressed in pink slacks and a deep rose sweater, she went back downstairs in a better frame of mind. She wasn't at all surprised to find her mother in the kitchen washing dishes while Dan drank a cup of coffee.

"Mother!" she protested. "You don't have to do that. Sit down and let's have a pleasant visit."

"Was there someone here besides the Millets?" Joan asked, her eyes filled with questions.

Jenna averted her gaze. "Curiosity killed the cat," she said evasively, trying to inject some humor into the worn cliché. The last thing she wanted to do was tell her mother the truth.

"There were four wineglasses," Joan persisted.

"Yes," Jenna agreed, "I suppose there were, but right now breakfast is much more important than last night's wine." Walking over to the sink, she took the dishcloth from Joan's hand. "Stop fussing about the house. I'll fix something for myself, and then we can sit down and visit."

She glanced at Dan, wondering if he saw how agitated she was. She hoped he attributed it to her desire for privacy; after all, that was why she had come here, and though she was pleased to see her visitors, their timing wasn't the best.

Dan grinned at her a little apologetically, and she had to smile. "You look remarkably well today, Jenna," he commented. "I believe you were right. Prout's Neck apparently does agree with you."

Trying to keep a blush from stealing up her neck to her cheeks, Jenna nodded. "I told you I needed the rest." But she knew that it was Brock's loving which had caused her to look so well. Despite its disappointing aftermath she had relished the time in his arms.

"Another cup of coffee?" she asked to change the subject. Dan agreed, and Jenna looked at Joan. "How about you?"

"Sounds good." Joan settled down in a chair next to Dan's.

Jenna brought over the coffeepot and sat down opposite them. Dan seemed extraordinarily restless, and Jenna guessed that he was eager to talk to her alone, but she ignored his meaningful looks and flattering words. She had enough on her mind today without adding to it.

The three of them drank coffee and talked for some time before Dan impatiently reached for Jenna's hand. "Why don't you and I go for a stroll along the water?" he asked.

Jenna saw no way to avoid the inevitable, but she really wasn't in the mood to deal with anything serious today. She had had enough of that last night. "Will you come, Joan?"

"No, I don't think so. You two go ahead. I believe I'll take a little nap. The drive tired me."

"Come on," Jenna coaxed. "The walk will invigorate you, put color in your cheeks."

"That's the least of my worries," Joan retorted. "I'd rather rest my bones." She laughed, and the sound was low and appealing, much like Jenna's laughter.

Even Dan's polite coaxing didn't persuade Joan, so Jenna was forced to give up. "All right. We won't be gone long."

"Have fun," her mother said. "Take your time."

Dan squeezed Jenna's hand. "Come on, let's go. I'm eager if your mother isn't."

Jenna was left with no choice but to make the best of things, and she decided that the walk really might be good for her. Dan smiled at her encouragingly as they strolled out onto the porch, and Jenna had to agree with him when he said, "I love this part of the country. It's still so natural, so quiet. A man can think here."

His words reminded her of Brock, and she hurried down the walkway, wanting to concentrate on something else. As they made their way along the leaf-strewn road toward the water Jenna could feel Dan's gaze upon her. When she glanced at him questioningly, his eyes glowed.

"You're very beautiful," he whispered huskily, leaning down so that his warm breath touched her face. "On stage or off."

Jenna brushed self-consciously at her hair, and she was aware that she wore no makeup. It didn't bother her to let Dan see her this way, not as it had with Brock, but although she was flattered by Dan's compliment, she would much rather have heard it from Brock.

When they had walked out of the woods, Dan unexpectedly drew Jenna into his arms and lowered his head. His mouth claimed hers before she realized his intent, and she felt chilled by his familiar touch.

She was reluctant to hurt his feelings, but she didn't want his kiss. His lips moved against hers urgently for a moment, and though he was an accomplished lover, Jenna remained passive. Feeling her lack of response, Dan moved away from her to stare down into her eyes. His hands remained on her upper arms, and he caressed her gently.

"It's still no good, is it, Jenna?" he asked solemnly. He didn't wait for an answer; he laughed in self-mockery, but there was real pain in his voice. "I came here to ask you to marry me. It troubled me as much as it did your mother to think of you up here alone, but I'm just daydreaming, aren't I? You don't need or want me to take care of you."

She was touched by his vulnerability and the futility of his dream, a dream so much like her own. Jenna reached up to trace his rugged jaw with a gentle fingertip. This was so awkward and painful for her; she tried to make light of the situation by saying, "I'm a big girl, and I don't need any man to take care of me."

But the sadness in her voice reflected the pain in Dan's eyes. He grasped her hand and held it to his lips.

"Oh, Jenna, don't tease," he pleaded.

"I'm sorry, Dan," she whispered, moved by his need. "I've told you before that I love you in my own way, but not as a prospective husband. I'm truly sorry. I don't—I can't—feel that way about you."

"It's still Brock, isn't it? And it always will be. It isn't fair, Jenna. I can't compete with a memory."

Jenna's lower lip trembled, and her fingers shook with emotion as she pulled her hand from his. "Don't do this, Dan," she murmured softly. "Don't back me into a corner. Let's not hurt our friendship with either/or choices." But she knew as well as he that he was right. She wasn't free to give herself to any other man because she could never escape from her love for Brock.

Fighting tears, Jenna began to walk swiftly toward the water. She couldn't bear to hear any more of Dan's declarations of love. It was embarrassing for them both. Then suddenly she stopped. Brock was sitting on a rock by the water's edge, and he was looking toward the shore. Instinctively fleeing the danger she sensed, Jenna started to retrace her steps, but it was too late. Brock had already seen them, though Jenna was sure he hadn't been able to hear their conversation.

Brock's eyes glittered, and he rose to leap agilely from one rock to another until he was on the shore. Jenna and Dan stood waiting as he sauntered toward them in that lithe way of his, and Jenna saw that Dan's face was twisted in disbelief as the blond man closed the gap between them.

"Dan," he said disarmingly, taking the initiative before the other man could adjust to his abrupt appearance.

"Brock! How the hell are you, man? What're you doing here? Where've you been?" Dan turned to look at Jenna incredulously. "Jenna, what's this all about?" he asked without waiting for Brock to reply to his staccato questions.

His eyes moved from one to the other, but Brock left Jenna

to offer an explanation. She began, then faltered, wondering why she hadn't made it easier for all concerned by telling Dan that Brock was here. "Brock—I—Brock was living at Solace when I arrived. He's staying with the Millets now," she added hastily.

"How convenient," Dan muttered with no small degree of sarcasm, and Jenna felt a rush of guilt well up inside her. Dan's moody dark eyes whipped over her. "Is that why you came here? To see him? You could have told me. I wouldn't have stood in your way, and I sure wouldn't have come here babbling like an imbecile."

"I didn't know he was here," Jenna protested. "Of course I wouldn't have come either, if I had known. Don't be angry with me, Dan."

"No, Dan," Brock drawled. "Don't be angry with Jenna. She wouldn't dream of hurting anyone." His words were biting, and Jenna was stunned by the magnitude of his bitterness as his gaze roved coldly over her. Only Brock knew the harshness was a futile attempt to deny the love he was feeling for her.

He had been shocked by his jealousy when he had seen Dan kiss Jenna, and he had been filled with an instant rage because this man had taken her in his arms. And yet he had no right to object. He had left her; she was free to do whatever she wished. The thought sent fresh anger surging through his veins.

How friendly were she and Dan? Had they slept together? The idea caused a spasm of pain to clutch at his stomach. He couldn't bear the thought of Jenna giving herself to some other man.

His eyes skimmed down her shapely figure, lingering on her full breasts. She was so appealing in the rose sweater, which outlined her tantalizingly. Brock knew her beauty only too well. He could almost feel her breasts swell to his touch now, the brown nipples rising to meet his teasing fingers, hardening under his thrusting tongue; he could taste her sweetness—but only in his memory.

He lowered his gaze. He knew just how well her hips fitted with his, and how they arched to permit him to enter her, sending a burning wave of fire through him as he explored her secret depths.

He knew the taste of her skin, the smell of it, sweet and scented with the fragrance of spring flowers. He knew the texture of her hair, the thick richness which a man could lose himself in. And as he remembered he felt a tightening in his loins; he ached for her now, and all the while his insides churned with jealousy.

He had counted on her needing some time to adjust to his absence in the past eleven months, but he had had no way of knowing what had gone on in her life. He had tried to keep tabs on her through his manager, but that was hardly satisfactory. He had tried harder to completely forget her. But that had been impossible.

"Brock was in an accident," Jenna offered lamely, uncomfortable under his intense scrutiny. She did not want to insult him, and she was acutely aware of the whiteness of his scars in the harsh daylight.

Dan stonily appraised Brock, and Jenna sensed her friend's confusion. "Well, aren't you going to tell me about it?" he demanded.

Shrugging offhandedly, Brock murmured, "What's to tell? I was in an automobile accident, laid up for a while, and here I am."

"Why didn't you let someone know?" Dan demanded. "We've all been concerned about you. Jenna especially."

Brock's thick brows arched ever so slightly. "Oh? Is that so? She didn't look concerned a few minutes ago. Was I mistaken, or were you kissing my wife, Dan?"

A flush crept up the big man's neck, and Jenna drew in an angry breath. The kiss might have seemed to be more serious than it was, but Brock still had tremendous nerve to comment on it, considering the circumstances.

"Your wife?" Dan asked tauntingly. "Your wife? Isn't that only a technicality?" Jenna winced at his harsh question. "Since when does a man simply vanish for eleven months and still consider a woman his when he decides to put in an appearance?"

Jenna held her breath as Dan's meaning seemed to sink in. She knew Brock's explosive temper well, but she wanted to hear what answer he would give to a question that had haunted her for too long.

The seconds ticked by as Brock glowered at Dan, one hand clenched into a fist at his side. Dan either hadn't seen Brock's injured hand or had discreetly ignored it.

"I knew I didn't have to worry about her," Brock retorted scornfully. "Jenna can more than take care of herself, and with . . . friends like you waiting in the wings, I knew she wouldn't be lonely." His eyes met hers challengingly. "Women like Jenna never are."

It wasn't the answer Jenna had wanted to hear, and it was plain that it had further angered Dan. "Why, you cold bastard—"

Unable to stand any more of the hostility and tension, Jenna took Dan's hand in hers. "Come on," she urged. "Let's go back to the house."

Dan's gaze was locked with Brock's, but when he looked at Jenna and saw the pleading in her pained brown eyes, he clasped her hand tightly and turned to follow her away. Jenna could feel Brock staring at her, but she wouldn't give him the satisfaction of seeing her distress.

"God, it was a shock to see him," Dan muttered in a low voice when they were out of hearing distance. "Good Lord, Jenna, why didn't you tell me he was here? I feel like such an idiot kissing you while he was watching."

"I'm sorry," she murmured contritely. "I didn't expect him to be at the cliff walk."

"But you did know he was here," Dan accused softly, his voice taut with displeasure. He walked rapidly, and Jenna had to hurry to keep up. "Why didn't you tell me?"

She didn't have an answer for him, and she was surprised

when he stopped abruptly and whirled her around to face him. "I *don't* have a chance, do I? I'm wasting my life waiting for you to get over Brock."

Jenna nodded, then looked away. Dan tilted her chin with his hand, making her eyes meet his. She could feel embarrassment color her cheeks. Only minutes ago Brock had once again made it clear that she meant very little to him, and yet she couldn't let go. She pulled Dan's hand away.

"I've tried, Dan." She laughed lightly, and the sound was mocking and mirthless. "But I can't seem to get him out of my system, no matter what I do. Like a fool, I keep hoping he still cares. Just to see him again—" Her soft brown eyes grew wide, and she shook her head again. "I'm really sorry. You know I am. I never meant to lead you on. My life has been so troubled, so uncertain since Brock left."

He nodded understandingly, but his mouth remained set in grim lines. "Yes, I know. I kept hoping that I could fill the void he left in your life. I wanted to be the one to make you happy again."

Jenna squeezed his hand. "You've been wonderful to me, and I won't ever forget it. Knowing you were there, caring, wanting the best for me, has helped me pull through some rough times, but seeing Brock again only makes me want him more." She licked her lower lip. "I honestly can't seem to help myself. He's running in my blood like a wild fever, and I'd rather have him, with all the pain and humiliation, than live without him."

Dan spoke in a surprisingly gentle voice. "You don't have to apologize to me, Jenna," he said softly. "In fact, I know just how you feel." He looked away, but not before she recognized his embarrassment. "I feel the same way about you. Jenna, honey, I'll take you on any terms I can get. Whatever happens with Brock now, just remember I'll still be here if you want me."

She looked at him with stiff determination. "Our situations aren't the same, Dan. Don't do this to yourself. There's no point.

Find some nice girl and make a life for yourself. Please, please don't put either one of us in this position."

His smile was sadly ironic. "Like you said," he murmured, his voice pained, "I'd rather have you—with all the pain and the humiliation—than live without you. I'll bide my time and see what happens."

"Oh, Dan, please don't be foolish," she implored. "Can't you understand? I have been—and still am—married to Brock."

"Yes, I know," he said. "Believe me, I know."

Drawing away, Jenna said more lightly, "We should get back to the house. Joan will wonder what's happened to us."

Dan started to object, then shook his head and followed reluctantly.

Joan was still sleeping when they returned, and they didn't bother to wake her. It was past lunchtime when she came downstairs. "Good afternoon. How was your walk?"

Jenna's quick glance at Dan asked him not to say anything. "The walk was all right. How was your nap?"

"Wonderful." Joan stretched. "I feel so refreshed. I haven't been sleeping well recently, but that nap really made up for it. Perhaps you do have a point about the rest here being better, Jenna. The house was quiet and peaceful, but you shouldn't have let me sleep so long. I want to spend some time with you."

"Obviously you needed the sleep, and we still have plenty of time to visit. How about some lunch? Are you hungry?"

"Yes, in fact, I am. Aren't you, Dan?" she asked.

He laughed. "I was born hungry."

"I'll make some sandwiches. Will ham and cheese be all right?" Jenna asked.

"That sounds fine, but let me do it," Joan offered.

"Nonsense," Jenna countered. "Sit down. Let me wait on you for a change. I'll have lunch made in no time." She looked at Dan. "I suppose you want another cup of coffee."

"You suppose right." He followed her as she walked into the

kitchen, and Jenna smiled at him. "I'm sure you know you drink entirely too much coffee," she said, trying to make idle talk.

"Ah, well, we all have vices."

"Don't we, though?" she murmured, and she couldn't help but think of Brock. If he wasn't a vice, she didn't know what was.

"Your mother loves you very much, Jenna," Dan said unexpectedly. "She's going to be disappointed when she discovers that Brock is back in your life. And she has to find out, you know."

"I don't know that he *is* back in my life. All I know is that he's here now. He might leave again at any time."

"Still—" Dan began, but Jenna didn't want to discuss Brock. She avoided Dan's accusing glance. "I wish I could get Mother interested in a man," she said seriously. "She's too much the concerned, doting mother. I love her, too, but this possessiveness isn't healthy for either of us."

"She only wants what she thinks is best for you," Dan assured her.

"I know that, but she needs to make a life of her own. Then she wouldn't be so wrapped up in mine. She should have remarried long ago."

"Who should have?" Joan asked, walking up behind them.

"You, actually," Jenna said. "You need to find yourself a man."

"I don't want one," Joan retorted sharply.

"And why not?" Jenna teased. "It would be good for you."

"So would some lunch," Joan said. "I thought you were preparing something."

"I am." Jenna turned back to the sandwiches, disappointed but not surprised that Joan wouldn't even entertain the idea of having a man in her life once again.

In minutes the sandwiches were made and neatly sliced in half, and Jenna placed them on a tray with a fresh pot of coffee and carried the tray to the living room.

Joan was curled up on the couch, absorbed in a magazine article. "What are you reading?" Jenna asked. "Lunch is ready."

Holding up the magazine, Joan asked, "Have you seen this piece on Evan Millet? It says he's the new Winslow Homer of Prout's Neck."

"No, I haven't read that magazine yet." Jenna set the tray down and wandered over to perch on the couch arm. "How interesting," she murmured, reading the piece over her mother's shoulder.

"Do you expect to see much of the Millets while you're here?" Joan asked, her eyes lighting up with interest. Jenna knew she had always been fascinated by Evan. "I'd love to see some of his paintings."

"Oh, I'd forgotten," Jenna exclaimed. "I told Martha that I'd come over for cards tonight. I'll run over and cancel."

"Don't cancel on our account," Dan insisted. "We'll start back early."

"It really doesn't matter. Martha's so informal. She won't mind, and we can make it another night." *And most definitely will,* Jenna added to herself.

"May Dan and I walk over with you?" Joan asked.

Jenna's eyes narrowed; she hadn't anticipated such a request, and she didn't want them to accompany her. However, it would be petty to refuse, and it would make Joan suspicious.

"Jenna?" Joan prompted.

"Of course."

"We'll go over after we've eaten," Joan said. "I'm well rested now, and I'd like the walk if you two would. Anyway, what else is there to do around here but take walks and visit people?"

Making herself smile, Jenna said, "I came here to rest, and you just told me a little while ago what a good place this is for sleeping." She glanced at Dan, and he raised his brows ever so slightly. Jenna knew what he was thinking, and she knew that she would have to tell Joan about Brock.

Joan returned Jenna's smile, then picked up a sandwich. "Yes,

I did say this was a good place for sleeping, didn't I?" she commented before she bit into the sandwich.

"Mother—" Jenna felt a certain urgency to get the unpleasantness over with.

"Yes, dear?"

"Brock—"

"What about Brock?" Joan interrupted, her posture immediately tense.

"He's here—staying with the Millets. You may see him if you go over there."

Joan tossed her sandwich back down on the tray, and Jenna could see that she was very upset. "What's he doing here? Have you seen him?"

This was just the kind of scene Jenna had hoped to avoid, and she sighed tiredly. "Yes, I have. He was in an accident, and he's here recovering."

"Oh, Jenna," Joan said impatiently, "surely you're not involved with him again." She pursed her lips angrily. "Haven't you learned your lesson? He's all too willing to start over now that you've made it, I have no doubts. He's a taker. Musicians—"

"Mother, I'm not involved with him again. Not really. And I certainly don't think he's eager to start over. Anyway, why must you always think the worst of him?"

"I *know* about men like Brock, Jenna," Joan said firmly. "I told you he was no good when you started seeing him. I told you it was a mistake."

Holding up a hand, Jenna murmured, "Please don't tell me again. I think it would be best if you waited here while I go to the Millets'. I don't want you getting distraught if Brock is there."

"I'd rather go if you don't mind," Joan countered.

Jenna looked at Dan again, but he didn't say anything. "Of course you can go if you wish," she replied, but it was the last thing she wanted. She did mind. Very much.

Lunch was civil in spite of the tension now in the air. Joan was distressed by the turn of events, but she made a determined effort to avoid the subject of Brock in favor of less explosive ones. Jenna managed to enjoy her guests; she found herself thinking that she was glad they had come, regardless of the situation. They were a welcome distraction from thoughts of Brock, and though the confrontation with Dan had been painful, it would have come eventually anyway.

The three of them dallied over the meal, talking about different topics, and it was easy for Jenna to suppress her nagging worries—easy until Joan asked, "Shall we go now?"

"If you wish," Jenna said, but she could feel her stomach tensing, and the food she had eaten was suddenly quite unsettled.

The three of them set out; the walk was invigorating, and they became quite congenial as they trudged through the bright fallen leaves, the wind breathing down on them with its frosty breath as the afternoon yielded to the approaching evening hours.

Dan walked between the two women, and Jenna didn't object when he linked arms with her and Joan. They engaged in light chatter as they worked their way through the woods, moving across the dry, rustling leaves of the maples and elms, but Jenna couldn't relax totally. She lapsed into silence as they approached the Millets' house, making their way up the path. Before Jenna could ring the bell, Martha opened the door and stuck her head out.

"What a nice surprise. How are you, Joan? Dan? It's been so long. Come on inside."

Jenna shook her head. "We only walked over so I could cancel our card game tonight. Mother and Dan are just down for the day." Jenna peered uneasily behind Martha, afraid that Brock would show up at any minute. She sensed Joan's discomfort and knew her mother was expecting the same thing.

"Oh, no," Martha said firmly. "You aren't canceling out. All of you come. We'll have a good time."

"Thanks, but let's make it another time," Jenna said.

"But I'd love to come, Jenna," Joan insisted. "That is, if Martha really doesn't mind two more of us."

"You're always welcome," Martha said. "I love company." She opened the door wider. "Do come in and speak to Evan."

"We won't disturb him now. We'll see him tonight," Jenna said. She was sorry Joan had agreed to come. She had much rather Joan and Brock had their first meeting without an audience, but it was too late now. She shouldn't have been surprised by her mother's easy agreement; it had been the opening Joan had wanted, she realized. The woman wouldn't be happy until she saw for herself just what she thought the situation was between Jenna and Brock.

"See you then," Martha said a little unhappily. She watched them go, then closed the door.

When Jenna reached the end of the walk, she impulsively turned to Dan. "I'll race you back to the house," she challenged.

He smiled at her. "You're on!"

Jenna began to run on flying feet, but it wasn't Dan she was trying to outrun at all; it was the future—and no one could escape the inevitable.

CHAPTER SIX

Jenna was dressed in an exquisite blue ruffled dress when she, Joan, and Dan arrived at the Millets' a couple of hours later. Evan greeted them warmly at the door.

"Jenna, come in!" He nodded to Joan and Dan. "How are you, Mrs. O'Neil? Mr. Newton?"

Although Joan waved a hand at him and smiled, Jenna knew that her mother was on edge tonight, anxious to see if Brock would be here. They hadn't discussed him further. "Please, Mr. Millet, call me Joan," she insisted.

"And call me Dan," the big man added.

Evan laughed. "You've made me an offer I can't refuse, and you must call me Evan, of course."

"We're honored," Joan said, giving him a generous smile.

Evan laughed again. "Don't be. I'm just home folk. A country boy from the hills of Kentucky. Now you folks come on inside. The others are already out back."

Jenna's heart began to beat a wild rhythm. The others, he had said, implying more than one. She found that her breath hung precariously in her throat as she trailed along behind the three of them, down the hall and into a big pine-paneled playroom. It was all she could do to maintain her composure when she saw Brock helping Dora Agate put paper plates and coasters in front of the chairs at a big round oak table.

Brock's eyes met hers, and though she felt unreasonably betrayed seeing him with the small, attractive blonde, she managed a facade of cheerfulness. "Good evening," she said brightly.

Dora turned around and gazed evenly at Jenna. Extending her hand, she said enthusiastically, "I'm so pleased to see you again. We weren't formally introduced the last time, but I'm a great fan of yours."

Wonderful, Jenna told herself dryly. *A fan of mine—and my husband's.* What was there to do but take the offered hand? She was sure that was a mocking look Brock gave her as he turned to the newcomers.

"Hello, Jenna," he said smoothly. "Joan. Dan." Resting an arm on the blonde's shoulders, he drew her forward a little. "This is Dora Agate."

Jenna heard Joan's sharp intake of breath, and she knew that telling her mother about Brock's accident hadn't prepared the woman for seeing him. Joan was staring at his scars, and Jenna was immensely relieved when Dora spoke again.

"This really is a pleasure. I'm pleased to meet you all." It took all of Jenna's willpower not to tear Brock's arm from around Dora's shoulders as she looked at them together. She was alarmed by the intense jealousy she experienced at the sight of Brock touching another woman. She told herself bitterly that it reminded her of a thousand other times and places, and she knew that her feelings for Brock hadn't changed; and she hadn't forgotten how possessive her heart was.

It should have been enough to convince her that Brock was right, there was no point in starting all that again, in trying to deal with those tumultuous emotions, but she couldn't help but wonder if he hadn't felt at least a slight twinge of jealousy when he had seen Dan kissing her earlier in the day. She was ashamed to find herself hoping that he had, that he still cared as intensely as she did.

Having no other choice, Jenna engaged in polite civilities. She could feel Brock staring at her and Dora, and she was irritated to think that he was comparing them. She wanted nothing more

94

than to spin on her heel and vanish, but that would have been all too easy. She found herself thinking that she and Dora were a study in contrasts, and that Brock had chosen an exact opposite for his next love. She had to concede that the two blonds made a very attractive couple.

Jenna steadied herself against a chair when Joan's eyes probed hers; her gaze was filled with anxiety and unspoken questions. When the woman looked at Brock, Jenna saw the hostility Joan felt for her son-in-law, and she saw something more, which she couldn't quite define, something that both puzzled and troubled her.

Joan's gaze settled briefly on Brock's left hand as it rested on Dora's shoulder; then she looked evenly into his eyes. "This is quite a shock, Brock. We've all wondered about you. You seemed to have disappeared from the face of the earth. We were—concerned." Her words sounded strangely loud and hollow in the hushed silence which ensued.

"Were you?" Brock asked coolly, and Jenna was reminded that there was no love lost between the two of them; it was a fact that had brought her pain too many times in the past.

"Brock was quite seriously injured," Jenna murmured, feeling the need to break the stifling silence which settled in again after Brock's question.

"And how long have you known?" Joan asked accusingly, her voice tinged with disbelief.

Jenna attempted a careless shrug. "I found out when I arrived."

She was ever so grateful to Dan when he rescued her by asking Dora, "Do you live in Prout's Neck?"

The pert blonde laughed infectiously. "No, I live in Portland, a short distance away. I'm Brock's physical therapist. He wouldn't come to me, so I go to him."

Dora glanced at Brock, and Jenna was sure she saw an intimate look pass between them. She had suspected that the thera-

95

pist and Brock were having an affair, so why did it hurt so much to see further evidence?

Locking her arm with Dan's in a defensive response, Jenna said too brightly, "Let's go find Martha."

As if on cue, Martha came into the room carrying freshly made pretzels and a jar of mustard. "Oh, hello," she called out happily. "It looks like everyone's here."

"What can we help you with?" Jenna asked, walking up to the plump woman. She cast an accusing glance at her friend; she felt that Martha could have told her Brock would be here with Dora, but Martha ignored the look.

"Nothing. Nothing at all. Sit down. Make yourselves at home. Evan!" she called, moving past Jenna and Dan to set the platter down. "Honey, get some bottles of beer, will you?"

Jenna stiffened her back, smiled at Dan, and seated herself in the nearest chair. Joan sat on one side, and to Jenna's dismay Brock chose to sit directly across the way.

Dora, settling down easily at Brock's side, gave her attention to Jenna. "I'm wild about that album *Hold Love Tightly*. You do a splendid job."

"Thank you." Jenna looked levelly at Brock. "Some of the credit must go to Brock. After all, he wrote the lead song for me."

When Dora smiled sweetly, Jenna looked for some sign of cattiness, but she didn't see any. "I didn't know that," Dora murmured, looking at Brock proudly. "It's such a moving song. The lyrics give me chills, especially the way Jenna sings them, as if every word comes from the heart."

Jenna forced a bleak smile to her lips. Every word did come from the heart—every time. "You're very kind," she said.

Dora was making it hard to hate her, not just because she was being so complimentary about the songs Jenna sang, but because the woman genuinely seemed nice. Though Jenna was intensely jealous, she was realistic enough to know that it wasn't Dora's fault that Brock made himself so available to her.

When Evan came bustling over with beers, Jenna was immensely relieved. Through a tall window she could see that the sun was sinking fast, and she shivered though she was inside. The air had turned cool, or was the chill only internal? Rubbing her arms briskly, she wished that she had hot coffee instead of beer, but she dutifully took a sip when Evan placed a frosty bottle in front of her. She was keenly aware of how quiet Joan had been since her comments to Brock, and Jenna turned to give her mother a reassuring smile.

Joan's attention was focused on Brock and Dora, and Jenna sighed wearily. She could almost see her mother's mind working: Brock and Dora. Perhaps things weren't as bad as she had imagined.

For Jenna they were worse. It was sheer agony to sit across from the man she loved while he catered to another woman. She felt like such a bitch, sitting there despising them both, but she was tormented by emotions she couldn't control.

Once Martha and Evan sat down at the table, things went much more smoothly. Martha was in command again, enlivening the conversation, making sure everyone was having a good time, bringing out the best in all concerned. Especially Brock and Dora, Jenna told herself. Jenna talked with Dan and Joan, Evan and Martha, anyone but Brock and Dora, although it was inevitable that at times she had to speak directly to them.

And it took all the strength she had. She thought of a hundred excuses to leave: She could say she had a headache, that Dan and Joan had to get back to Boston, that she had left something in the oven, but she knew that she would use none of the excuses. She would sit across from her husband and another woman while her stomach churned and her heart ached, and she would pretend to be having a good time.

At last the card game got under way, and Jenna found herself toying with the hundred excuses again. Surely she wasn't going to sit here and endure several hours while they all played cards.

She didn't even enjoy the game; she had learned because Brock liked the challenge. Now she shouldn't care what Brock enjoyed, but pride wouldn't permit her the luxury of running away. One hour dragged by, then two, while Jenna sat between Joan and Dan and pretended great interest in her hand or the bidding as game after game came and went.

Jenna glanced across the table more than once to find Dora helping Brock hold the cards in his injured hand, insisting that he use it to keep it flexible, and every time the woman touched him, Jenna cringed and wished she didn't have to endure the sight of the two of them, so blond, so close together.

At last she could use an excuse which sounded plausible. When a game had ended, she looked at her watch, then stood up abruptly. "We'd better be going. I hadn't realized it was so late."

At that moment the phone rang. "Just a second, Jenna," Martha requested, pushing back her chair. "Let me see who that is. Now, don't leave."

Dropping back down in her chair, Jenna awkwardly awaited Martha's return. They all looked toward the hall when they heard a whoop of laughter coming from the other room. They exchanged amused glances and waited for Martha to return and tell them what had caused her excitement.

Her face was glowing when she rushed back into the room. "Evan!" she cried excitedly. "That was Jud. He got married! Married, Evan! He's seventy-eight years old, and he just married a seventy-three-year-old woman. They're back in the States, and they'll be coming here tomorrow."

It seemed to take Evan a moment to digest the information. Then he rubbed his chin. "Well, I'll be damned," he murmured, shaking his head in wonder. "That old son of a gun!"

"I think it's wonderful," Jenna said. "I hope they'll be very happy."

"It's grand!" Martha exclaimed. "I've always said that marriage isn't the perfect state, but it beats the hell out of being single."

Jenna carefully avoided Brock's gaze. "As I said, we'd better be going."

She stood up again, and Joan and Dan followed suit. They all brushed aside their hosts' protests that it was still early and they should stay longer. When they had thanked Martha and Evan for the evening and given Dora and Brock a curt but civil good night, they stepped out into the chilly New England air.

Jenna's breath escaped in an audible sigh of relief. "I'm glad that's over with," she muttered.

"I can understand why," Joan agreed, but Jenna knew that she didn't understand at all. "I can't abide Brock Hanson, and I don't know why he had to come back here of all places."

Jenna bit her tongue to keep from defending Brock. She and her mother had gone over all this too many times, and besides, Brock no longer needed Jenna to defend him. He wasn't hers to defend, and there was no longer reason to hope that Joan and Brock would ever become friends.

"We really should get under way," Dan said. "That drive back to Boston takes a couple of hours, and it's after eleven now."

"Of course you'll stay the night with me," Jenna insisted. "I just wanted an excuse to leave here."

Dan shook his head. "I honestly do have to get back. I have to audition a group at ten in the morning, and I don't want to be too tired to see if they're what I want for the club. We hadn't planned to stay the night."

"But it's too late to go now," Jenna objected.

Joan reached out to grasp her daughter's arm with unnecessary force. "Come back to Boston with us, honey. Surely you don't want to stay here now. Brock will only upset you. You won't get any rest at all."

Without replying Jenna started walking down the sidewalk. She was sorely tempted to do just as Joan suggested. Staying here would only cause her more pain, but she knew she couldn't go until this thing with Brock was resolved with some degree of finality. Or had it already been?

"I'm only staying a few more days," she told her mother. "I'll give you a call when I'm ready to return to Boston." She began to walk faster, but Joan wasn't going to give up so easily.

"Jenna, you know how unhappy this makes me. I thought all that business with Brock was over. I hope you're not doing this out of pity for him. Obviously he's finished now as a pianist, but that's not your problem. We've—you've worked too hard for what you have to get stuck with Brock again. He'll only cause you unhappiness."

Jenna was embarrassed to discuss this in front of Dan. "Mother, I don't pity him! Now please don't quarrel with me about it. Don't put me on the defensive about Brock. We've discussed this all before. You don't understand."

"I understand all right," Joan replied bitterly. "I've understood about these things since your father—" Her hand tightened on Jenna's arm. "Believe me, Jenna, I know what you're letting yourself in for. Don't give him the chance to hurt you again."

"Joan," Dan interjected, "you can't live someone else's life for them. You can't protect Jenna from pain. She'll have to make her own mistakes."

Jenna noticed his slight emphasis on the last word, and his eyes, when they met hers, held a trace of pity. Jenna looked away.

"Please," she cried in exasperation, "I don't want to talk about Brock anymore. Let me work it out for myself."

Brock gazed after his wife long after the door had been closed on her retreating figure. Dan had been the one leaving with her instead of him. "Damn," he swore under his breath. He had promised himself a hundred times that he would let her go, that he wouldn't become involved with her again. They had only to be in each other's presence for all his old wounds to bleed again. But he'd be damned if he wouldn't rather hurt with her than without her.

He wanted her; he couldn't help himself, no matter what he said. He ached for her, desired her. He had to have her again, if only for long enough to force her out of his system, but even as he told himself that, he knew it was a lie. It wasn't just physical desire he felt for her; his soul hungered for her. He loved her.

He knew there was no use fighting with himself. He wasn't really ready for a new commitment; and there was still the matter of his career, but he couldn't wait for that now. Jenna was back in his life. He would take a step at a time and see if there was anything left to salvage of their relationship. He would see if he could convince himself that she didn't pity him; that they still had a chance to make it as man and wife. Otherwise he would do what was necessary: divorce her.

"Brock." He looked up to find Dora smiling gently at him. "It's your turn to play."

A sheepish grin moved across his lips, and then he laughed aloud. He hadn't even remembered that he was playing cards. Shaking his head, feeling like a fool, he glanced at his hand and saw that the high card was the queen of hearts.

Jenna was sitting alone in the living room, lost in thought, gazing blindly at the dancing flames of the fire when she heard a knock on the door. Joan and Dan had been gone for over an hour, and she couldn't imagine who would be calling. Gathering her sweater more tightly to her body, she crept quietly to the front door.

She cursed because Brock had never gotten around to installing the peephole he had promised her. Then she smiled grimly to herself. That wasn't Brock's responsibility now. If she wanted a peephole, she would have it installed or do it herself.

"Who's there?" she called firmly, hoping her voice didn't betray her agitation at receiving a late night caller.

"Brock," came the equally strong response.

"Brock," she repeated in a hoarse whisper. Before she thought about what she was doing, she had flung the door open. She was astonished to see her husband on the doorstep with a suitcase in hand.

Her eyes raked down his lean body, silhouetted against the darkness by the light spilling from the doorway. "What are you doing here?" she demanded, a frown distorting her lovely features.

His gaze was defiant as he made a studied appraisal of her. "Moving back in."

She opened her mouth in surprise, then quickly recovered her composure. "No, you're not!"

"I didn't come to argue," he said flatly. He walked toward her, and short of using physical violence Jenna didn't see how she could bar his entry.

Still hanging on to the door with one hand, she turned to stare at him. "I told you I'd be out in two weeks. Can't you wait that long? We agreed to that, didn't we?"

He shrugged carelessly, then set his suitcase down. "I don't recall. You have a way of making everything fuzzy for me, Jenna." He smiled slightly, and Jenna felt a foolish rush of warmth flood her body.

"Why are you here, Brock?"

"I told you. I'm moving back in."

"Why? Why don't you stay with the Millets until I leave?"

Brock gazed evenly at her. "Would you have me put a honeymoon couple out of their bed? Jud and his new bride will arrive tomorrow."

"Oh." She brushed at her long hair nervously, knowing that he had a point. Or was she looking for any excuse to have him here with her? She didn't know what to say, but she knew that either he or she would have to find another place to stay. This wouldn't work at all. She sighed tiredly; he had been here first, so it was only fair that he be allowed to have the house.

"All right," she murmured. "I'll move out in the morning. It won't matter if I cut my stay short."

Their eyes met and held. "Why leave?" he asked. "We both own this house, and I think it's large enough for the two of us for a few days, don't you?" He didn't wait for her to answer. "You stay out of my way, and I'll stay out of yours. That won't be too difficult, will it?"

Jenna's mouth felt incredibly dry, and she licked her lips. It sounded damned difficult to her; in fact, it sounded impossible, but she didn't want to own up to that. She lowered her gaze, avoiding his steady, penetrating scrutiny. "No, I guess not."

"Good. After all, it won't be the first time we've stayed here together." He swiftly turned to close the door. Jenna's fingers touched his as he removed her hand, and she had a foolish urge to clasp them. When the door had been shut, he picked up his suitcase. "I'll take the green guest room. I'm sure you're settled in the master."

"Yes," she murmured, "but—" Again she looked away. She had wanted to tell him not to take the green room, for it was right next to the master, but, of course, it was larger and more comfortable than the yellow guest room.

"But what?"

"Nothing." She couldn't make herself say it. She was being silly. It wasn't as if she had never lived in this house with Brock, and it *was* half his. But things were so different before. So very different.

"Good night."

"Good night," she murmured, still stunned by the turn of events. She honestly hadn't anticipated his returning while she was here. It had been his idea to move out. She watched him walk up the steps without a backward glance, and when he had vanished, she trailed slowly behind. She wouldn't torment herself by exploring the implications of his being here in the house with her. A picture of Dora flared in her mind, and she gritted her teeth. Surely he wouldn't allow the woman here now!

Suddenly she was aware of every sound as her ears automatically strained to listen for Brock's movements. She could hear him settling into the bedroom next to hers, opening drawers and rearranging hangers in the closet. Finally she became conscious of how tense she was, standing there like a fool, focusing on Brock's every move. Turning away in disgust, she marched toward the bathroom and ran some water in the tub. A bath would relax her, she was sure.

After she had stripped off her clothes and put her hair up on her head, she sat down in the tub with a sigh of contentment. Then she became aware of the shower going in the other bath. Brock was bathing, too, and for some reason it seemed so intimate to think of the two of them nude, the water caressing their skin.

Her mind began to drift as she imagined Brock under the stream of water, his magnificent body and golden hair wet and glistening. Not so very long ago they had showered together in that same room. A blush stained Jenna's face bright red as the memories flamed to life in vivid detail. She and Brock had often made love in the shower. She felt a yearning deep down inside her, followed by an intense hunger in the most womanly regions of her body as she recalled those torrid times of their loving.

Brock had the power to stir her to life as she had never imagined any man could. He was skilled, sexy, and wondrously male; when he drew her against his demanding body, she opened up to him like a flower seeking the rain so necessary to sustain life.

"Jenna, you fool!" she muttered aloud, scattering the memories which were so powerful and visual that her body was actually responding to them with a flooding warmth. "Stop it!"

She grabbed a cloth and soap and began to scrub her body vigorously, the harsh movements an attempt to purge herself of the pictures which clung stubbornly in her mind, made all too real by the man in the room next door.

When she had washed every inch of her much too roughly, she dried on a thick towel, then went over to her closet. There were so many beautiful clothes there that it was difficult to select a robe. Finally she settled on a red satin one Brock had given her for Christmas.

She tied the belt securely before going over to her vanity to sit down. For a moment she gazed at her reflection, seeing the dark eyes, the high cheekbones now pink from their brisk scrubbing, her well-shaped nose, shining and freshly cleansed, and her sensuous lips devoid of any lip color, but naturally rosy.

Reaching up, she freed her hair from the clasp which secured it high on her head; she let the dark masses tumble down in waves around her shoulders. Then, her brush in hand, she began to stroke her hair, giving it the same thorough treatment she had given her skin.

When her arm grew tired, she tossed the brush down on the bureau. She poured some scented lotion into her palm and grimaced as she smelled the faint sweetness of gardenia blossoms; she couldn't abide them now that she knew the scent was worn by Dora Agate. Scooping the lotion back into the bottle, she took another brand.

She perched one long shapely leg up on the edge of the vanity chair and began to smooth the lotion along the curving length, feeling the silky richness of her skin. She sensed that someone was watching her, and she became still as she looked in the mirror at her bedroom door. She had left it open without realizing it, and she saw Brock standing there, looking at her. Her eyes widened as they met his in the mirror, and she lowered her leg to the floor, partially covering it with the red satin robe, which slipped to expose some of her thigh.

She was alarmed to feel the excitement brewing inside her with the knowledge that Brock had watched her. "What do you want?" she asked in a breathy voice, tensing visibly. She had meant to sound angry, but she hadn't managed to hide her heightened awareness of him.

He leaned back against the doorframe, and Jenna saw that he was in a short brown robe, his muscled legs and finely arched feet bare except for their covering of thick, curling golden hair. He smiled lazily at her, then spun the liquid around in the brandy snifter he held in his hand.

"I'm not sure. What are you offering?"

He was playing with her, and Jenna bit down on her tongue to keep from offering herself. "Nothing."

"Then I guess the question is academic." He took a sip of his drink. "I just dropped by to see if you needed . . . tucking in."

Jenna sat before the mirror, still gazing at Brock's image there. She was unable to turn around and look at him, afraid he would see how his nearness excited her, sending the blood rushing to her head.

"I'm getting ready for bed," she stated, although it was all too obvious.

"Alone?"

"Of course alone," she retorted. Did he think she had some man hidden in here? she asked herself. Why was he here at all? Did he want her, or did he enjoy her discomfort? She was sure he recognized the effect he had on her.

"Pity," he murmured. Did Jenna hear a trace of regret in his voice, or had she only wished it were there? Could it be that he did want her, that he was suffering the same agonies, the same insecurities she was? She watched as he pressed his lips together, then tipped his head in her direction before he left her, disappearing down the hall with deliberately casual steps.

When Brock had closed the door to his bedroom, his thoughts went unerringly to the sight he had just seen. He had never known a woman more appealing than Jenna. She was a rare package: talent, determination, intelligence, and beauty. Oh, so much beauty. He felt a quickening somewhere deep inside him, and he told himself that it was funny how the thought of her making love to another man had so easily erased all his determination to keep her out of his life.

Perhaps, he told himself, it would be worth the pain and humiliation to spend a single night in her arms, satiating body and soul for just one more time. It would be worth it to hold her, to see her satisfied smile after they had shared each other.

"You're an ass, Brock," he said aloud. Then he laughed because he knew it was true, and the admission didn't change anything. There was still the past, still the problems, and still the future—all wrapped around Jenna.

Jenna clenched her hands into fists, arched her neck, closed her eyes, and drew in a deep, steadying breath. This wasn't going to work. She couldn't stay here with Brock. He was tormenting her, and she would never be able to survive it. She made herself walk over and shut the door, and then she pulled off her robe and slipped under the covers of the king-size bed. The bed she had once shared with the man in the next room.

For a long time she lay in the dark, listening to Brock as he stirred about. And she wondered if he didn't have at least some of the same yearning she had to touch, to share, to talk, to make love. She rolled over on her stomach and hid her head under the pillow, and she was terribly conscious of how her breasts ached and her hips were pressed against the firmness of the mattress. Twice Brock had rekindled the flame of desire inside her, and twice he had left it burning. Surely he had been moved by their kisses—excited as she had been.

Apparently he hadn't, she told herself unhappily, for after a few minutes the door to his room was firmly closed and the restless movements she had heard in the room ceased; she was sure she could hear Brock's deep breathing. Or had she only imagined it because she couldn't get to sleep herself? For a moment she lay staring at the blackness, bitterly regretting the wall which kept her from her husband, the wall which was more mental than physical.

She tensed when she heard the door to her room open, and she glanced at it just in time to see Brock enter. Then the door closed again, and she was left in the darkness, knowing that her hus-

107

band was coming relentlessly toward her, hidden in the blackness.

Unable to move or speak, Jenna held her breath. Brock didn't turn on the light and neither did she. She heard the soft rustle of clothing, and she knew that he had removed his robe. Without saying a word he eased his hard body down on the bed and slipped beneath the cover.

Jenna's breath was locked in her throat as he drew her against him, her naked body warm and yielding as it met the hard lines of his. She wanted to protest, to insist that he do something more than just claim her, but she couldn't. She wanted him too desperately to ponder the circumstances or reason the right or wrong of making love with him again like this after all the months and the bitterness.

There was a sense of urgency in his movements, as though he were coming to her against his will, and Jenna felt a rush of guilt as she submitted to his rough kiss. His mouth came down on hers punishingly, but she didn't turn away.

She sensed the fever burning hotly in Brock, for it burned as hotly in her, a fever too long raging in her veins with no relief. Only Brock could cool it. Jenna's entire body was afire as he lay on his side, embracing her with his right hand, holding her to the long length of him. His fingers moved burningly along her curves, caressing as a man too long alone would.

Involuntarily Jenna's hands traced Brock's well-defined body, her fingers outlining muscles and entangling in thick, curling hair until they had explored his strong maleness. She heard his tormented groan as he drew her more tightly against him, and she slid her hands around his hips, holding him to her.

His kiss deepened as though he couldn't get enough of her, and she moaned in need, wanting him as never before. Their separation had been too painful and depriving, and they both had waited too long for this time in each other's arms. Their passion was running like wildfire, and there was no stemming the tide of their desire.

Firmly easing her onto her back, Brock lowered his body to Jenna's. There in the blackness of the room, without a tender word, he took her, his loving fervent and unrestrained, and Jenna could do nothing to stop him, for she wanted him as desperately and uncontrollably as he wanted her. He drove into her soft depths like a man obsessed, and Jenna met his powerful movements, arching her hips, wanting to feel his every thrust deep inside her.

Brock gathered her possessively to him; he wanted to pierce her so deeply that she would never again love anyone but him, never want anyone but him. He wanted to touch her heart and soul, so that she would always be his.

Wrapping her arms around him, holding all that she had wanted so achingly for the many long and lonely months, Jenna gave herself to Brock with an abandon that was almost shameful. She wanted to become so much a part of him that he would never again be able to hold another woman in this way without thinking of her.

Their bodies burned against each other, their desire raging out of control as they were consumed by the blaze. The flames of their passion rose higher and higher until they exploded with love's hottest fire. At last Brock and Jenna lay in each other's arms, overwhelmed by the intensity of their hunger, breathless in the aftermath of their desire.

Jenna felt a sudden loss when Brock moved away from her to lie silently by her side. She wondered if his heart was pounding as furiously as hers, his body throbbing with the afterglow of their love, his soul crying for words of love and promises about the future.

When she felt him slip away from her, she lay in the darkness, watching a shaft of light flare brightly, then die as the bedroom door was opened and closed. Brock was gone as quickly as he had come, stealing Jenna's heart and her love, and leaving her hurt and confused, and so totally alone in their bed.

CHAPTER SEVEN

It was very early in the morning when unfamiliar sounds began to seep into Jenna's consciousness. She struggled to free herself from the shackles of the dark night and the darker dreams which had haunted her. Scenes from last night rushed to her mind, bringing with them shame and embarrassment as she recalled the way she had given herself to Brock, then been left alone.

She chafed irritably at the memory as she began to awaken more fully. In her partially drugged state she imagined that she heard the faint strains of piano music. She was sprawled across her bed sideways, her hair strewn over her face like a mask. Tugging at the bedraggled strands, she brushed them away so that she could focus her eyes.

Sliding back against the headboard, she pulled the covers up to ward off the morning chill. God, she felt awful. Suddenly she held her breath. There it was again, the teasing, drifting notes of the piano. Brock! He was practicing. She was sure of it.

She listened for a few more minutes, then slipped from the bed to pull on her satin robe. She felt a tightness in her throat as she very quietly made her way down the hall to the music room. The door was shut, and she furtively eased it open the slightest bit.

Brock was sitting before the piano in his robe, his eyes closed as he worked something out in his head. The room was cocooned in the last shadows of night as daybreak tapped at the wide windows. Jenna felt a flush creep up her body at the sight of

110

Brock, but she held her breath as she silently watched him deal with the magnitude of his frustration.

His good hand moved across the ebony and white keys, skillfully seeking out a melody, but the injured one poised and quivered, an unwilling prisoner, refusing to be the instrument of Brock's mind. Brock kept trying patiently, so patiently, to manipulate the stiff fingers, the scarred hand, but it was virtually locked in position.

He was repeating the words of the song over and over as he tried unsuccessfully to make his hands cooperate. Jenna marveled at his fortitude. The Brock of old would have slammed down the cover and stalked out in a temperamental fit.

As though Jenna had willed it, Brock suddenly raked his useless hand along the length of the keys and then pushed both hands down with all his strength, causing the keys to give a last hoarse protest.

Jenna felt the tears rise to her eyes, and she began to stealthily back away; she'd rather die than be discovered watching Brock at such a vulnerable time. However, she didn't manage to escape before she saw him slam down the cover, then slump forward, resting his elbows on it in bitter defeat.

On flying feet she fled to the bedroom before Brock could see her. She couldn't get the sight of him out of her mind. He both tormented and haunted her, and she found herself thinking that she could help him compose if only he would let her. She swept away the thought; of course Brock wouldn't let her. He had too much pride, and she respected him too much to offer. The situation was difficult enough as it was.

She was sure he could be as good as ever at his song writing if only he would accept his damaged hand and adjust to his handicap. It would require more patience and more practice, but eventually he would learn to compose with one hand. Other artists had done it.

Weary, troubled by what she had seen and by memories of the

night before, Jenna pulled her robe off and sought refuge in her bed. In no time she fell into a deep, fitful sleep.

She was teased awake much later by the soft rapping which tugged at the edges of her consciousness. "Jenna. Jenna, are you asleep?"

Surprised to hear Brock's voice, soft and coaxing as he called her name, she quickly hopped out of bed and put on her robe. "No," she called, hurrying to the door. She opened her eyes wide, trying to rouse herself before she saw him. After last night she honestly wasn't sure what to expect. She brushed at her hair and smoothed down the robe, wishing suddenly that she had been up and dressed.

She opened the door to find Brock clad in brown slacks and a beige sweater. His eyes moved appraisingly over her figure, then returned to her face. "Would you be interested in going to Portland with me this morning?" he asked.

He so startled her with the question that Jenna was at a loss for words. Her eyes registered her puzzlement. He had said nothing at all about last night and the way they had made love so wildly and passionately. She began to wonder if she had dreamed it.

"What do you say, Jenna?" Brock murmured, and she gazed into his eyes. They held hers, and though Jenna could read nothing in the expression, she wondered if Brock wasn't as embarrassed about last night as she. Was this his way of starting over more slowly?

"I'll treat you to a late breakfast," he offered with a lazy smile calculated to make Jenna's heartbeat quicken. "Sticky, gooey sweet rolls and steaming black coffee."

His choice of breakfast fare brought a faint smile to her lips. It was what she had served Brock their first morning together. At the time, it had been all she had had in the house, and, anyway, she had a weakness for bear claws dripping with melted butter. The memory was too sweet to ignore, the chance to spend time with Brock too tempting to turn down. She smiled more fully.

"Is that a yes?"

"How can I refuse such an offer?" she murmured, but she was filled with both hesitation and excitement. She was in the mood for anything but light banter.

Brock had come to her a dozen other times right in this very room with that same offer, but it hadn't been after an eleven-month separation culminating in a night of intense love. She wasn't sure what any of it meant, but before she could start the endless and futile speculations, she shoved her thoughts aside. The man had asked her to breakfast, and she had accepted. So far there was no more to it. It could mean good news, and it could mean bad. Only the day would tell.

"I'll get dressed," she said. Brock stayed a moment longer, and Jenna felt uncomfortable. She was suddenly shy with him, not wanting him to see her change clothes. After a teasingly short time he turned and walked away.

Jenna rushed to her closet to gather up charcoal slacks and a soft gray sweater, then hurried to put them on. When she gazed at herself in the mirror, she was tempted to exchange the outfit for the most attractive clothing she owned, but she resisted that bit of foolishness. *Be sensible,* she chided. *Be sensible.* This was not cause for celebration; for all she knew, Brock might want to discuss the divorce today.

She tried to hide the anticipation shining in her eyes when she joined him downstairs. "I'm ready."

"So you are," he said, his smile telling her he found her appealing.

Her gaze skimmed down his attractively clad body, noting how the brown slacks outlined his muscled legs so enticingly. *God, but he's handsome,* she told herself, and she smiled with a casualness she was far from feeling.

She wanted to kick her heels gleefully as they headed for the car, but she walked quietly by his side, making polite chitchat about the morning and the last clinging leaves defying the autumn winds. Brock's comments were equally harmless. They both appeared calm and at ease, and Jenna wondered if Brock was churning inside as she was, brimming over with excitement and turmoil at their unexpected togetherness. She couldn't help but question his reasons for this outing. Not only was he taking her to breakfast, but he was being friendly and charming. His behavior reminded her of the special times in their past, and she fervently hoped that the day wasn't going to be a big disappointment.

The short ride to Portland was uneventful, and once Brock and Jenna had finished their breakfast of sweet rolls and coffee, he invited her to go shopping with him. He needed a new suit, he informed her lightly. She agreed just as lightly.

Shopping with Brock had always been an experience, and Jenna had always sworn that he was choosier about his clothing than she was about hers, and that said a lot. This time was no different. At least in this realm he hadn't changed, she told herself as she watched him try on suit after suit at the first men's clothing store. He didn't find anything he wanted, and finally he grinned at Jenna.

"Let's go, Jen," he said.

She found herself foolishly examining his every word; he had called her Jen for the first time since he'd come back into her life. She glowed as she walked out into the sunshine. The day was brisk, and a chilly wind was blowing, portending winter, but she felt oddly warm and happy. She couldn't control her optimism, no matter how she tried. She was here and Brock was here, and it was almost like old times.

Almost. Surely they could work something out; surely they both had learned from their mistakes. Brock wouldn't punish her because his hand forbade him to continue to perform. He couldn't. He still cared for her; she sensed it in the way a woman does those things. They had once been such a big part of each

114

noon, she procrastinated, trying to think of the best way and time. She had to know. Jealousy or no jealousy, she had to know how much Dora meant to him.

Hours later, when they had settled down to watch a television program, Jenna found what she considered the proper time to question Brock. He had drawn her against his side and was nuzzling her neck when she murmured, "Brock, I want you to tell me about your relationship with Dora. You were certainly with her longer than an hour."

Brock pulled away from her immediately, and Jenna heard a disgruntled sigh escape his lips. She could sense his chagrin, and though she felt guilty about bringing up one of their old conflicts, she could not give herself to him if Dora was really part of his life now. Their eyes met, and Brock shook his head.

"I wasn't with Dora all that time. I had some business to attend to."

"What business?" Jenna asked curiously.

"Nothing important." Brock shrugged, then effortlessly changed the subject. "As far as Dora goes, she extended herself to me at a time when I wasn't willing to try—or even cooperate. She laughed and smiled and made me see that none of what I was going through was as bad as I thought it was." He made a wry face, and Jenna could see his admiration for the petite blonde.

"She works with people much more severely injured than I am." His gaze was steady and firm when he looked at Jenna. "I consider Dora a friend, and I don't intend to give up that friendship, Jenna. This is part of what we were talking about yesterday."

There was no challenge in his tone, only a weary recognition of what was an ongoing problem between them. Jenna tensed, knowing in her heart that she never wanted Brock to see the other woman again, but knowing exactly what he was saying and why. "Are you sleeping with her, Brock?"

She held her breath as she saw his lips turn down at the corners. Then he ran a hand through his thick blond hair. "No."

Jenna licked her lips, aware that she should stop at that admission, believe him, and go on from there. But she couldn't. "Do you know that she wants to sleep with you?"

His midnight-blue eyes glittered angrily. "How do you know? Did she tell you?"

Averting her eyes, wishing to avoid the pain which inevitably came with these confrontations, she shook her head. She didn't even know where she stood with Brock yet, and trying to find out about Dora's place in his life was unbearable. "No, but I can see the way she looks at you."

"And a blind man could see the way Dan looks at you. Are you sleeping with him? Will you ever see him again at all now?"

Jenna looked at Brock in surprise, but his point was well taken. She gave him an embarrassed smile. "No, I'm not sleeping with him, and yes, I would like to see him again. He's been a good friend to me."

Brock drew her back to his side. "But we understand each other now, don't we, Jenna?" he murmured. "I don't particularly like your . . . friendship with Dan, and you don't like mine with Dora. But we need other people in our lives besides married couples. Both of us have to stop feeling threatened by the attention someone else gives one of us. If this is going to work, we have to trust each other. We can't keep repeating the same destructive patterns. Right?"

She raised her eyes to look at him, and when she saw the intensity of his gaze, she touched his cheek lightly with her fingertips. "I love you, Brock. There's never been anyone else for me but you. I'm possessive, I know, because I'm so afraid of losing you, but I'm trying in every way I can to let you know that I want a future with you, not just another beginning for our marriage. I can't take the constant partings and reunions."

He kissed her fingers as they traced his lips, then murmured against them. "I know, Jen. I know." He lowered his head and gently kissed her mouth, his lips clinging slightly as he drew away. "I love you," he whispered huskily. "And I want to believe that we've learned enough in these past months apart for that love to see us through the hurdles."

Jenna thought about the song she was going to record, and she hoped desperately that Brock would remember his words when she told him. But somewhere inside her a tiny voice cried out that he would never understand, that this would be one of the hurdles that would put a newfound and freshly trembling love to the test—maybe even shake it to the core.

CHAPTER NINE

The next several days were ones of both joy and pain for Jenna as she and Brock nestled in their private haven at Prout's Neck, rediscovering each other, talking about things past and present, and making love.

Jenna was almost afraid to believe that they had found each other again. She wasn't fool enough to think that their marriage was on solid ground by any stretch of the imagination, but she knew that the stronger the bond formed between them at this point, the better able Brock would be to see that she only wanted to help them both by recording "When Love Is Gone."

Without a career Brock would never be content. Jenna knew he was searching for something which would drive him, compel him, to create as much as the piano had, and they both knew no miracle would reconstruct Brock's hand so that he would be able to play again.

Dora, in all her optimism, agreed that Brock would regain some use of his fingers over the months to come, but never to the extent that he could stroke the piano keys as he had in the past. He would never play professionally again; he would be fortunate if his unyielding fingers would work sufficiently for him to use both hands to compose at the piano.

Jenna was convinced that she was doing the right thing in recording "When Love Is Gone" when she returned from an hour at Martha's house, where she had gone to get her copy of the tape and had been practicing. She walked into the den to find

Brock working with the model ship again. He had been going back to it more and more often as the days passed, and Jenna knew that he was growing restless, though he tried to hide the fact. She had encouraged him to compose on several occasions, but he had spurned the idea, and she knew he couldn't remain idle indefinitely. She saw how frustrated he was as he attempted to cement the tiny kevels to each half of the ship's hull. She saw how futile his attempts were because of his injured hand. Hesitating a moment, she finally decided to try to help him.

"Hello," she said cheerfully. "What're you doing?" She walked over to stand beside him, and he glanced distractedly at her, a frown on his face.

He hadn't expected her back from Martha's so soon, and he hadn't wanted her to see him trying to work with these damned little parts. He needed time alone to find out if he could succeed at anything besides loving her. Once he had spent hours working with these models, but now it was so defeating that he could hardly stay at it for more than a few minutes. It was just so pointless. He couldn't hold on to the small parts, much less place them where they should go. Two good hands were needed, and he only had one.

"I'm putting this ship together." He stated the obvious, taking his frustration out on Jenna. He hated for her to see his weakness at anything.

"May I help you?"

"No, I'd rather do it myself."

"Why?" she asked.

He looked at her again, his blue eyes stormy, but he didn't answer her.

"I could help," she persisted.

When he didn't respond, she said gently, "Brock, don't shut me out. The relationship won't work if we can't talk, if we can't help each other. You're punishing yourself doing this kind of thing."

She gestured toward the ship and the tiny parts lying on the

149

table. "You need two hands, and I'd like to help you. In fact, I'd enjoy building the ships with you. It'll be fun. Please let me help."

Brock seemed to weigh her words. Silently he held out the kevel to her as he slid over so that she could join him on the bench. When she smiled at him, he managed a faint smile in return. Jenna could see that he had his doubts about accepting her help; he considered it a weakness. But as they began to make some progress on the model he relaxed visibly.

Jenna realized that it was only his hobby he had agreed to let her help with, but it was another chink in the armor he had built around himself. His career was an altogether different matter, of course. Could he bend enough to let her help with that too? She seriously doubted it.

She hadn't approached him about her trip to Boston because she knew that it, too, would be a touchy matter. She would not let him go to the studio with her, of course—not that she thought he would want to. She would explain that she needed to spend some time with her mother and she hoped that he would remain at Solace for a couple of days. There were matters to be resolved, and her mother was really one of those, though hardly the only one.

Jenna and Brock were sitting in front of the fireplace, watching an old movie on television and eating popcorn, when she mentioned the matter of going away for a couple of days.

"I need to go to Boston tomorrow, Brock," she said, hoping he couldn't hear the pounding of her heart.

"To Boston?"

She nodded. *Don't argue,* she pleaded silently. *Don't make it any more difficult than it already is.* She saw the curiosity in his eyes, and she wondered if he had learned to trust her enough to let her go.

"What for?"

"I should tell my mother about us."

Brock nodded. "Yes, I guess you should."

Jenna looked at him, a little surprised that he had agreed so easily, too easily, she found herself thinking suspiciously. She brushed the thought away; she had enough to worry about without making up things, and she knew she should be grateful that he had agreed so readily.

"Will you be able to keep occupied?" she asked lightly, knowing she was hunting for some sign that he hated to see her go.

He looked at her a little strangely, she thought. Or had she imagined it? Then he smiled, and his voice was teasing when he spoke. "Oh, I think I can find a little something to occupy myself."

"Just make sure it's by yourself," she said lightly, hoping her tone didn't reveal the extent of her insecurity.

He tapped her chin playfully. "Don't make your brown eyes green," he said, easily perceiving her jealousy. "Actually I have a few errands to take care of."

Jenna wondered what they were; she wanted to ask, but she didn't want him to press her on her trip to Boston, so she kept quiet. Unexpectedly Brock ruffled her hair playfully, then took her by the hand. "Let's go to bed," he said.

Jenna forgot about tomorrow as she walked with Brock up the steps. He eased her down on the bed, then lay by her side. "I thought we came up here to sleep," she murmured as he gazed longingly at her.

"There's a time and place for everything," he returned, reaching for her. Jenna's lips parted under the pressure of his, and she gloried in his passionate kiss. She seemed to grow more hungry for him each time he took her in his arms.

He drew away from her to unbutton her blouse, and she sucked in her breath when his mouth played provocatively over one breast. He traced the shape of it, his tongue making smaller and smaller circles until it licked at the waiting nipple, and Jenna moaned with pleasure and drew Brock's head down more firmly against her. He gave the same attention to the other breast, then scattered warm kisses over her skin, down the valley between her breasts, and lower until he reached the waistband of her slacks. Jenna raised her hips and helped him take off the rest of her clothing. She watched as he turned off the light.

When he had undressed, he produced a small vial of scented oil, and Jenna smiled in anticipation. Many were the times they had smoothed oil on each other, and she sighed contently as Brock began to massage her skin. The oil was warm and fragrant, and her skin tingled slightly as Brock's large hand made caressing circles down her throat, over her breasts and stomach, and down to her long legs. When he had languidly massaged the length of them, he had Jenna turn over, and he caressed her back and derriere, working the oil into her skin with long, gentle strokes, warming her, stirring her desire for him as his hand roved and and teased.

At last he handed the bottle to her, and Jenna took great pleasure in running her hands over his crisply curling hair, massaging his well-defined chest and abdomen, stroking his muscled, hairy legs. When he rolled over on his stomach, she paused a moment to admire his broad shoulders and lean, muscled buttocks. His masculinity had the power to make her breathless, and she bent over him, administering to him with the utmost delight.

After she had smoothed the oil on all parts of his body, she settled down on the bed beside him. Brock lowered his muscled body over hers, and she put her arms around him to caress his naked back, her hands playing down low on his hips, tracing his masculine form. Brock arched against her, his throbbing love for her evident against the softness of her curves, and she drew his hips to hers as she locked her legs around his waist.

She sucked in her breath as he moved against her, slowly filling her with the wonder of him, and she gasped with pleasure as he began to make his special magic, his rhythm slow and driving. She drew him tighter, holding him and the moment, glorying in his ability to carry her away to that exquisite palace of passion where desire and pleasure danced as one to the melody of unchained love.

Love's dance gradually became faster and faster. Jenna held on to Brock, matching his movements, whirling and spinning to the increased tempo as she listened to the crescendo of her heartbeat. Suddenly their mounting ecstasy reached its height in a wild explosion of joy; then they gradually gave way to the sweet strains of violins as the song and the dance slowed and ended.

Jenna smiled contentedly as she waited for the thunder of her own heart to lessen and her breathlessness to ease. She lay in Brock's arms, sheltered by his love, as she waited for the deep sleep that often came after the intense joy.

"Good night, my darling," Brock murmured in a deep, satisfied voice.

Jenna lightly kissed his cheek. "Good night, Brock."

For the trip to Boston, Jenna chose jeans, which she rarely wore, and a navy-blue sweater. The jeans hugged her shapely figure, making her look leggy and quite young. She braided her hair into a single plait and let it hang down her back. She intended to go to the house in town and change into something more feminine for her session because her attire altered her mood. She wanted to look her best for Brock's song.

She had slipped the tape into her purse, and she hoped to be able to practice the song some more on the way into the city. The mere thought of recording it sent chills of excitement up her spine and just as rapidly sent a shiver down it. What if Brock hated her because of what she was doing? What she thought she was doing for them? What then?

She gave herself a final glance in the mirror, then left her troubling thoughts in the bedroom as she went downstairs, being deliberately cheerful. Brock, dressed in jeans and a maroon ribbed sweater, which made him look so manly that it took Jenna's breath away, smiled lazily at her but said nothing. She wondered if there was something behind that enigmatic smile, but she merely returned it.

"Well, I guess I'll be going," she said lightly.

"Yes," he agreed easily. "The morning's well under way." Going over to the closet, he took a coat out for her. "You'll need this. It's chilly out."

She glanced at him anxiously. He seemed almost eager for her to go, and she couldn't stop the doubts from pouring into her mind unchecked. What *was* he going to do while she was in Boston? She battled with an image of him and Dora, and she bit down on her lip nervously. They had gone through all that yesterday, and she had to trust him, but that didn't ease her mind.

Knowing she had to get to the studio, she forced the unpleasant suspicions from her mind. Brock opened the door for her and walked with her to the car.

"Have a safe trip," he told her. Then he reached over and kissed her briefly on the mouth.

"I'll see you in a couple of days," she murmured.

He nodded, then opened the car door for her. "Have a nice time."

With an overwhelming feeling of unease Jenna climbed in and started the car. She couldn't back out now. Everything had been arranged at great cost and difficulty, but she was sure that if a trip to see her mother was really all she had planned, she would have changed her mind and stayed home with Brock.

Brock watched Jenna leave the driveway, then hurried back into the house. He didn't have time to waste today; he had somewhere to be. Pulling a coat from the closet, he slipped into it. He went upstairs for his new suit, and when he had taken it from the bedroom, he hurried down the hall. The sight of his piano caught his eye, and for a moment he stared at it, wondering if he was making a mistake. Suddenly he was shaken with doubts about what he was planning. He had known when he saw Jenna in the living room crying after they had made love that he had to do something. He couldn't risk hurting her again. But was this

154

really what he wanted? What if it was another mistake? What then?

When Jenna reached Boston, she took a few minutes to stop by the store where her mother still worked as a clerk. Jenna had been glad that Joan hadn't given up the one thing in life which kept her busy just because Jenna could—and would—have supported her. She had bought a new house for Joan, and she could have well afforded for her mother to retire early.

The smile on Joan's face made Jenna feel guilty, as it had often done since she had become so busy with her career. Her mother always seemed to make her feel that she had been a neglectful daughter, and Jenna found herself dreading the confrontation over Brock.

"Jenna, baby, how are you?" Joan cried, rushing out from behind the counter where she was writing up a sales ticket. "Excuse me," she told the customer. "This is my daughter, Jenna O'Neil, the famous singer."

Joan began to rattle off the titles of her daughter's songs while Jenna stood beside her in embarrassment, wondering if the customer was any kind of music fan or was being bored to death by Joan's prattling.

"Now, Mother," she said gently, "I'm sure this lady doesn't have time to listen to tales about me."

The woman smiled brightly. "Oh, I've heard your songs, and you do sing beautifully." Her eyes raked down Jenna, taking in every detail from hair to feet.

"Thank you," Jenna said sincerely, smiling warmly. She turned back to Joan. "I'd like to take you to lunch at noon if you haven't made other arrangements. I'm going to be in the recording studio today."

"I'd love to, Jenna. You know that," Joan said. She turned to the customer. "Would you mind terribly if someone else helped you?"

"That's not necessary, Mother," Jenna scolded. "I'll see you at noon, and we'll decide where to go from there."

"Really, I don't mind someone one else helping me," the customer said quickly.

Shaking her head in exasperation, Jenna watched as Joan persuaded a shy little clerk to finish the sale. Then, locking arms with Jenna, she drew her aside. "Where shall we eat today?"

"Let's pick a little out-of-the-way place. I'd like to talk with you." This time Jenna's eyes met her mother's meaningfully; there was no way out.

Joan's face twisted into an unhappy mask as her suspicions grew. "Not about Brock. Don't tell me that's the reason you're taking me to lunch. Oh, Jenna, come to your senses. Don't start all that pain and misery again. You've been through enough."

"When we go to lunch, we'll discuss it," Jenna said, her tone brooking no argument. "And, Mother, try to keep an open mind. I love Brock, and I want to make a good marriage with him."

"It's not possible, and you know it," Joan said harshly, her words laced with disgust.

There it was again, that inexplicable hostility which had always seemed unreasonable, but Jenna didn't have time to worry about it now. She gave her mother a warning look, sighed unhappily, and said she would see her at noon. When Jenna reached the house, she had only enough time to change and practice Brock's song once more. She freed her hair to hang around her shoulders in appealing waves. Then she chose an attractive crimson dress and complemented it with tall heels.

She was almost late getting to the studio. The band was already there, tuning their instruments, and Jenna, unusually nervous, went over to talk with them as Jake got the orchestra established. The place was in pandemonium, and Jenna was unaccustomed to working under these conditions, as were the musicians. Finally things settled down enough for the rehearsal to begin, and Jenna breathed a little easier. It looked as if everything might possibly work.

After three hours had passed, Jenna was drained. She was sure that everything had gone as well as could be expected under the circumstances, but all concerned seemed ready to pull their hair out—especially Jake, who generally had the patience of a saint. When the lunch break rolled around, Jenna was more than ready for a breather.

She picked Joan up at the shop, and they drove to a tiny Italian restaurant across town. They were seated at a little table far in the back by a waiter who knew and respected Jenna's need for privacy, and after they had ordered, Jenna started right in trying to explain that she and Brock were going to make their marriage work.

"Why?" Joan cried plaintively. "Why, when you have everything? Success. Money. Fame. *Respect.* Why are you so determined to put yourself back in his grip again? Do you enjoy punishment, Jenna?"

"Because I love him," Jenna replied simply. "Because all of it—money, fame, success—isn't worth as much to me as being Brock's wife."

"My God!" Joan murmured in a long-suffering voice. "I thought you'd learned your lesson. Don't you know he'll destroy you? Warp your entire life? Even I can see that he'll be worse than ever now. He's just a has-been piano player. He'll live off you—your fame, your success. He'll go through your money—"

"Stop it, Mother!" Jenna commanded sharply, her voice low and tense. "Brock doesn't need to live off me. He's a composer. Good heavens, don't you realize that if he took his share of the money from 'Hold Love Tightly' alone—which he wrote, I'm sure you recall—he'd never have money worries again? He could live the rest of his life off that one song if he managed wisely. And he's written another which will be an even bigger hit. Oh, Mother," she said, "why must you continue to despise him? Don't you care that he means happiness to me?"

Joan sobered at the blunt question, and Jenna saw the woman struggle for composure. "I don't want to see you hurt anymore.

I don't want to see your life ruined. I told you from the beginning that he would hurt you. I knew it when you told me he was a musician. And a piano player at that."

"You've always been unfair to Brock. You seem to hate him because he's a musician, and that's hardly a good reason."

"Musicians are moody, self-centered, and care only about their work," Joan retorted.

"*I'm* a musician," Jenna declared. "I care about something besides myself. Why do you persist in believing Brock can only bring me disaster?"

A faraway look came into Joan's brown eyes, and Jenna gazed at a woman she was sure she had never seen before. "Don't you want what's best for me?" she asked, trying to draw Joan back from wherever she had gone in her mind. "What is it that you *do* want?"

Joan reached across the table and clasped one of Jenna's hands. "I've done everything in my power for you," she said fervently. "I've lived my entire life for you."

"I love you, and I appreciate all the love and time you've given me, but to care for me to the exclusion of all else was wrong." Jenna could feel her voice falter but felt compelled to continue. Her thoughts had been bottled up for so long, now that she had begun to put them into words, she didn't seem able to stop herself. "You shouldn't have given up your life for me. I didn't ask you to, and it wasn't fair to either of us. Let me go. Live a little yourself. For heaven's sake, I'm twenty-eight years old."

Releasing Jenna's hand, Joan clasped hers together and looked down at them blindly. Tears welled up in her eyes, and Jenna felt as if she to were about to cry. But she also felt relieved somehow, having said so frankly what had needed to be said for so long. "I'm sorry, but I want what's best for both of us," she murmured. "You're still a young woman. You deserve a life of your own. I do, too, and I want Brock in my life. It hurts me that you despise him so."

"What have I done?" Joan whispered, tears slipping down her

pale cheeks to splash on her locked hands. "Where did the years go?"

Jenna drew both her mother's hands to her lips and kissed the wet fingers. "You did what you thought was best. I'm not blaming you, Mother. You've loved me, and you've worked hard—too hard—for me, but we have to do things differently."

Joan shook her head. "I hadn't realized until now that I never intended to let you go. I don't despise Brock. I despise the artist in him."

"But, Mother—"

Joan slid her hands away from Jenna's so that she could grip the edge of the table. "You and I have needed this talk, Jenna." She looked deeply into her daughter's brown eyes. "I should have told you the truth long ago, but somehow I just couldn't. It hurt too much to remember."

"Remember what? What are you talking about, Mother?"

"Your father was a piano player. He—" She lowered her gaze. "He never married me, Jenna. He's still alive and knows about you. His name is Drummond . . . Drummond O'Neil."

Now it was Jenna's turn to grip the edge of the table. She was stunned. Shocked. She watched as Joan's face flamed a bright red, and she saw the fingers clutching the table tremble.

"Drummond was a struggling musician when I met him. He felt that he couldn't afford a wife and baby, so we didn't get married. I used his name when you were born, but he never let me legally make it mine. He became more and more successful, and less and less interested in me—in us."

Jenna saw the fierce pride flame in her mother's eyes. "I began to hate him because he never wanted me. He would have taken you, later, when you were older, but I forbade him to see you to punish him. I hated him so by then that I only wanted to get even with him."

She began to cry quietly, and Jenna went around to the other side of the table to draw her into her arms. "My father didn't give me a dime," Joan murmured. "In the days when you came

159

into the world as an illegitimate child, it was still considered sinful. I was eighteen years old. Father disowned me. My mother was dead. I didn't know what to do. Because of shame and dishonor I felt I had to leave Providence, where we lived. So I moved with you to Boston. I took a job in the same store I still work in. I told everyone that I was a widow. It was just you and me, Jenna."

Jenna hugged her mother, then sat back down in her chair, her legs weak. "You should have told me long ago," she whispered. "How awful for you."

"Father died a few years later, and I inherited what money and possessions he had because there was no one else. I gave you music lessons and encouraged you because Drummond was your father. I wanted you to make it in the world, Jenna. I wanted to prove that we could be somebody too."

Her eyes again met her daughter's. "Drummond used me. Then he made a new life without me. He didn't care if I lived or died. He was driven, obsessed with his career, and he's done very well for himself in California. He climbed over everyone he could to get ahead."

"But you say he's heard about me?" Jenna murmured.

"He never wanted a thing to do with us," Joan said solemnly. "Then he heard your song and saw that you really had talent, and all of a sudden he was proud of you."

Jenna was shocked. She couldn't believe that after all this time she had a father. That he was alive and knew about her. All these years she had thought her father was dead. Now that she did know about him, all she could think about was her mother and the pain she had suffered. "I'm so sorry, Mother," she murmured. "I wish you had told me long, long ago. It sounds like you must have loved him very much at one time."

"I worshiped him. He was my life. I would have died when he abandoned me if I hadn't had you."

"How could you have kept it a secret all these years?" Jenna asked.

"I never found the right time to tell you. Then it didn't seem to matter. You were happy. You were successful. Drummond shunned us, but your talent made you a star. And I loved you for being successful. Somehow I felt that you had vindicated me although Drummond hadn't wanted me. Then you became entangled with Brock, and I saw my life repeating itself in yours."

"No," Jenna denied. "The only similarity was that we both fell in love with musicians."

"I'm sorry, so sorry," Joan whispered. "I lost my way, Jenna. Can you understand that? I lost my way. I wanted—" She held out her hand and shook her head. "I don't know what I wanted anymore."

Stunned by the magnitude of Joan's revelation, Jenna murmured soothingly, "It doesn't matter now. You did your best for me, and no one can say it wasn't a good job." When Joan looked away, Jenna ordered, "Look at me, Mother."

Joan's tearful brown eyes slowly met Jenna's. "We'll begin again, you and I. You must let the past go. Don't waste the rest of your life. You still have me, but you need more than that. Meet other people, take part in life."

"I'm afraid," Joan confessed, her lower lip trembling. "You're the only person who's never hurt me. I don't know how to live any other way."

"I'll help you, just as you've always helped me," Jenna said softly. "You need a change, a new career. You have to start living again. Travel. Make friends."

The food arrived, and Jenna was immensely grateful for the waiter's sensitivity. He discreetly served them without a word, then vanished as quickly as he had come.

Jenna stayed longer than she had meant to, and she had to hurry once more to get Joan back to the store and then make it to the studio for the second half of the session. She didn't know if she would be able to sing; the secret her mother had revealed seemed incredible. Yet, it was all true. Her mother's words rang in her head over and over. Suddenly the pieces began to fall into place; her mother's seemingly irrational dislike for Brock, her possessiveness.

When the time came for Jenna to sing "When Love Is Gone," she made several false starts; she was perilously near tears before she got herself under control. She wasn't a temperamental artist in the studio, but today she was a bundle of emotions.

Jake took her aside and talked with her a few minutes, and eventually she was able to try again. Miraculously she managed to forget what her mother had told her at lunch long enough to sing her song. She was feeling vulnerable and defensive, and it turned out to be a tremendous plus for an already sensational song. Today Jenna could bleed as easily as Brock must have done when he wrote the lyrics.

The ordeal was grueling and prolonged, with first one thing then another going awry, but Jenna knew when it was right. She realized that she had never sung with such intensity, such pain, such personal involvement as she had today. Right on cue she heard Jake exclaim, "We've got it," and she knew from the excitement in his voice that he wasn't sorry she had insisted upon adding the song to the album. "When Love Is Gone" was sure to be a tremendous hit.

After it was over, all Jenna wanted to do was collapse. She thanked all involved, declined her band's offer to go out for a drink, and wearily headed toward her house.

In the silence of her car her mother's face came back to her, and she recalled what Joan had said. Her father, alive. It simply didn't seem possible.

There had been no pictures of her mother and father, and Joan had rarely mentioned the man, saying only that he had died right after Jenna had been born. The mention of his death always seemed to stop all questions, for Joan had said it in such a manner that one was reluctant to pursue the subject. Jenna had thought that it must have been dreadful for her to have been widowed so young and to have no one.

There were no friends to talk of either Jenna's father or Joan's.

162

But that hadn't been unusual in today's society, and in view of the fact that Joan had moved to Boston from Providence, it was even less unusual. Jenna was feeling confused and down when she inserted her key in the door and stepped into her living room.

Her hand flew to her mouth, and she stifled a gasp when she saw Brock sitting on the couch. "Brock!" she cried. "What are you doing here?" Her eyes raked over him as he sat there in his new suit, a glass of wine in hand, listening to some music on the stereo.

He shrugged carelessly. "I missed you," he said lightly, but Jenna could sense that there was more to it than that.

She was shaken by his presence; she didn't know what it meant, and she had been under so much pressure already today. She wondered how he had gotten in, and as if he were reading her mind, he held up a door key.

"I still had this, and you weren't home, so I decided to use it."

She nodded and unconsciously ran a hand through her hair. "Bad day?" he asked.

Jenna forced a smile to her lips. "Certainly not a good one." She stared at him, wondering what he would say if she told him about her day. She had almost forgotten the possible repercussions of what she had done. For sheer survival purposes she had reached a point where she had only wanted to give a stunning song her very best, then be left alone to deal with her mother's disquieting news.

She didn't tell him, of course, and as she gazed at him she saw the tenseness around his mouth, the tired look in his eyes. "What really brought you into Boston?" she asked. She had a sudden need to unburden herself of her mother's secret, but she didn't feel the time was right.

"I thought we could go out to dinner," he said. "You look beat, and it might be good for you. Want me to run some bath water for you?"

Deep within her Jenna knew that there was more to Brock's

being here than a desire to take her out to dinner, but she agreed. "That sounds like a good idea."

"I could even wash your back," Brock added with a wicked smile. Clearly he was trying to reestablish the intimate mood they had shared at Prout's Neck.

The faintest of smiles flickered across her lips. "That would be nice. I really am beat."

Brock tossed his coat onto the couch and rolled up his long-sleeved shirt to the elbow. "Your every command is mine to obey." He gave her a mocking bow and left the room.

He was teasing her, but Jenna sensed a certain tension beneath the banter. Still, he was here, and she had to admit that she was glad to see him. She needed him tonight.

After undressing and pulling on a robe she went into the bathroom, where she found a tub full of fragrant warm water and frothy bubbles, as well as a glass of chilled wine on the tubside table. Brock watched as she wound her hair up in a knot on top of her head and then slipped off her robe. She blushed under his frank and admiring gaze. As she slid into the water she sighed; it enveloped her tired body like a cocoon, and she closed her eyes and lay back against the high tub back.

She partially opened her eyes to look at Brock as he took a cloth and soap and began to bathe her legs, holding up first one, then the other, resting them on his arm while he washed and massaged, aiding the circulation, driving away the deep aching Jenna was experiencing.

"Mmm," she murmured, closing her eyes once more. "That feels heavenly."

"Be careful what you say," he replied. "You'll get more than a bath."

She smiled at him. "I'm too tired for anything more."

"And tonight it'll be a headache," he joked, causing her to giggle.

Brock laughed, and for the first time that day Jenna felt a special thrill as the sound washed over her. He began to bathe

the rest of her, and she discovered that she wasn't quite as weary as she had thought. His slightest touch had always been sufficient to arouse her passion, and her skin flamed under his hands. Jenna wondered if he was aware of the effect he was having on her.

"How hungry are you?" he asked.

"Very."

"Good. I didn't have any lunch, so I'm starving. We'll really do the town tonight. I think we both could use the distraction. I had a tough day too."

"What happened?" she asked, dying to know why he was here in Boston.

Brock smiled slightly and shook his head. "Nothing much—yet."

"You're not going to tell me," Jenna accused. He had a secret he was keeping from her; she was sure of it, but then, she reminded herself, she had one of her own.

"I'll tell you later," Brock promised. "In my own time."

Jenna had to be satisfied with that, at least for the time being, but her curiosity was almost unbearable.

"How did it go with your mother?" he asked in an obvious effort to change the subject.

Looking at him cautiously, almost as if she imagined that he had guessed her secret, she murmured, "Not too bad."

Jenna saw her mother's tearful face again in her mind's eye, and she was sad because Joan was so lonely. She wanted the three of them to be a family, but she didn't know if it would happen. The thought suddenly reminded her that she had a father, a very real and powerful one, and she had no idea how she really felt about that. It was so unreal she almost felt as if she had imagined it. She was still in shock, she guessed.

Would it change her life to know she had a father and that he had deserted her and her mother? She suspected that it wouldn't. He hadn't wanted her or her mother. He knew who she was, but out of either guilt or fear he had chosen not to contact her, even now that she was an adult. He had never made a move to amend the mistakes of the past. She sighed. She felt it was best that way, but she realized she was still overwhelmed by the news: she wouldn't try to think it out now.

She smiled at Brock, took a sip of wine, then climbed out of the tub. He was holding a huge bath towel out to her, and when she moved forward, he wrapped her in it, picked her up, and carried her to the bed.

She forgot that she was weary. She forgot that she was hungry. Even that she had a father. She knew only the moment and Brock as she stretched out before him, her beautiful body still glistening with water. She watched as Brock discarded his suit and walked toward her, the hungry need and desire all too evident in his eyes.

CHAPTER TEN

After the loving, Brock murmured to Jenna, "I've made reservations for dinner." He mentioned one of the most exclusive places in Boston. "It was no easy trick to get in on such short notice, so we'd better get dressed and get over there."

The time in Brock's arms had made Jenna forget her earlier disquiet, and now she sensed that the evening would be full of excitement. Brock's enthusiasm, as well as his mysterious refusal to tell her his news, only added to the feeling, causing her to dress as quickly as possible. In less than half an hour she had dressed in a gold lamé gown and gold heels. Her hair hung loosely around her shoulders, its darkness framing her face and adding luster to her gown.

Brock whistled long and low when she went into the living room. He had been dressed for fifteen minutes and was reading when she came in. "You look especially lovely tonight," he told her, his eyes glowing.

Although she had a dozen things on her mind, not the least of which was the afternoon's recording session, she gave Brock all her attention as they drove to the restaurant. There was a liveliness, a suppressed energy about him which she hadn't seen in a long, long time, even before they separated, and she was eager to know the cause.

They were led to a beautifully decorated table in the center of the massive room, and Jenna was mildly surprised that Brock didn't protest the table's exposed position, for he had never been comfortable being on public display while he dined. She, on the other hand, had always loved people too much to object, and even though it often meant an interrupted meal, she didn't mind. She realized that her husband was making a concerted effort to change the old Brock. Perhaps he had discovered at last that he couldn't hide forever. He had to begin to live a normal life, and if he was going to stay with Jenna, that meant a life in the spotlight.

"You look like a woman in love," he murmured low as he gazed across the table at her.

She smiled. "Maybe that's because I am. And you look like a man with a secret," she accused. "What is it? The suspense is dreadful."

"It's good for you," he teased. "Helps keep you on your toes."

"Oh, Brock, tell me," she insisted. She was beginning to become more anxious than curious.

He smiled, and she saw the excitement dance in his blue eyes. "Later."

"Is it good news?" she pressed.

Brock looked down into his glass of wine for a moment, then met her eyes. "I think so, but I can't be sure yet. We'll have to wait and see."

Brock laughed gently, and Jenna saw a woman at the next table give him an admiring glance. It pleased her inordinately to once again find herself in public with him. It had been far too long. She had the foolish urge to turn to the other patrons and say, "Look. It's Brock. He and I are back together."

They ordered lobster, and Jenna settled back in her chair, anticipating the sumptuous meal she knew would follow. She had dined here several times before, and she had never been disappointed.

After the salad arrived, she began to eat, enjoying the tangy house dressing. She tried her best not to let her mind stray to the disturbing news her mother had given her, or to worry about

Brock's response when he learned the truth about what she had done today.

She would tell him in good time, in her own way, after the newness of their togetherness had worn off, but certainly before she did any of the promotion work on the record or it came on the radio.

She would have to be ever so careful how she handled this sensitive matter; she knew in the dark corners of her mind, where fear cast its ugly, threatening shadow, that Brock would be livid at first, no matter how delicately she announced what she had done, but she hoped against hope that he would see that she had done it for them both.

"Jen?"

She raised her eyes to meet his. "Hmm?"

"I said I love you," he murmured. "But you were so lost in your thoughts that you didn't hear me. Penny for them?"

She smiled brightly. Her thoughts were worth so much more than a penny. A future, perhaps, a lifetime. "I was thinking how fortunate we are to have a second chance. Some people aren't afforded that luxury."

His face was solemn. "We would always have had that chance, Jenna. I didn't know it myself, but I was waiting for the right time—a time when I could come to you again, offer you what you deserve."

She shook her head, pained by the implication of his words. "You have only to give me yourself, Brock. You and I lost almost a year of time, and to lose any, when none of us knows how much we have, is such a waste of a precious commodity."

He nodded. "But I've explained to you that I have to live with myself before I can live with you."

Jenna reached out and took his crippled hand in hers. Brock tensed slightly but did not pull away. "I love you so much, Brock. I would have done anything to get you back."

"Well," he said suddenly, "I don't suppose there could be a

better time than right now to tell you my news. I wanted the moment to be just right, you know?"

Jenna nodded wordlessly, wanting him to hurry and tell her.

"The thing is, Jen, that I came into Boston today in order to make a demo of 'When Love Is Gone' and another song I've been working on called 'One More Time in Your Arms.'" His eyes burned with blue fire, and Jenna could feel her heartbeat running wild.

He couldn't have! It wasn't true. It couldn't be. But she knew from the shine in his eyes that it was.

"I had Turner Rhodes do it for me and a couple of musicians from the old days. They all thought it was good, Jenna." He shrugged a little uncertainly. "I knew the time had come when I had to try. And I think I was right. I took the demo to Paul, and he thinks I have something too. He's a good manager. He's stood by me not knowing if I would ever do anything in the business again. He wants to see if Austin Lane will record them both. Austin Lane, Jen. You know what that will mean if he does. I'll be in as a songwriter, really in. And I won't have done it by riding on your name." His eyes were so very solemn when they gazed into hers. "I couldn't handle it if someone said that was the reason I went back to you."

Jenna had known despair so often in the recent days and weeks and months; now it was washing over her again, causing her stomach to tighten, her head to ache. She forced a smile to her mouth, and when it quivered dangerously under the threat of tears, she licked her lips.

Brock placed his hand over Jenna's, and she could feel his surging excitement. This was the break he had wanted. This was the chance he needed. And he had done it on his own, as he had told her he would.

And she had just added his prize song to her album. Without asking. Without permission. All at once she wanted to make today go away. She wanted to have heard this news yesterday and been wild with joy about it. She wanted to sob her heart out.

170

She wanted to explain. She wanted to comment, but she was struck absolutely dumb by his news.

"Jen?"

She could see the disappointment, the uncertainty, in his eyes as his excitement paled in the face of her apparent uninterest. She would never know where she found the strength to speak. "It's wonderful news, Brock. I'm just so stunned. I never imagined— never dreamed—and Austin Lane, the hottest male vocalist of the year— It's all so marvelous. Congratulations."

He squeezed her hand. "It's not in the bag yet. Austin hasn't even heard the songs, but Paul thinks he'll want them." His eyes were glowing with pride. "It's a new life for me, for us. I believe I can make it now, and that's all I needed to know."

He suddenly looked sheepish. "I sound like a damned young fool making the football team, don't I? It was just so crucial to me, so damned important that I can't begin to tell you. This hand—" He freed it from hers and held it up. "It did something bad deep inside me, for I realized how I associated my life, my image of myself, with my music and my career. A man isn't just who he is—he's what he does, too, and I had needed this hand so much to do what I wanted. But now I feel like I'm alive again, in control again, like something as basic and vital as my manhood has been given back to me." He looked away from her. "I wish the food would come," he muttered. "I'm sounding like an ass."

"No," she whispered. "You sound splendid. You sound like you've found yourself again, Brock, and I'm so happy for you. I know what pain you've known, for I've known pain too." *And will again,* her mind screamed.

There was a pause; Jenna was unable to go on, for she was afraid that she would lose Brock again when she told him what she had done. Why had it never occurred to her that Brock would want someone else to record "When Love Is Gone"? He had written it for her; he had told her so. But she took small comfort in that now. She had intended to tell him that she thought he meant for her to have it, as he had "Hold Love Tightly," but now she couldn't even say that.

The words of "Hold Love Tightly" rose like a litany to haunt her. She couldn't be in this much trouble with such good intentions, could she? Could one single day really be slapping her in the face so many times? Was this man across from her the one she had made love with an hour ago?

For a crazy instant she thought of calling Jake and telling him that it was all a mistake, that he should take the song back off the album. But how could she? That hurried session today had cost them thousands of dollars—an awfully big price to pay for a decision made in foolish haste. Her head began to pound ominously, and she felt sick to her stomach.

"Are you all right, Jen?"

Why did Brock's voice sound so far away? She glanced over at him and realized that she had had her eyes closed. "Yes, fine. Wonderful, in fact." She made herself smile. "But I'm so hungry. My stomach is all in knots. Excuse me for a moment, will you, Brock?"

Without waiting for his response she raced to the ladies' room, ignoring the surprised and pleased looks as she was recognized by some of the patrons along her path. She barely made it to the restroom in time. She had never been so sick in her life. She didn't know what to do. She was trembling like a leaf, and her insides were in turmoil. She had to make a decision, and fast, but she simply wasn't able to.

She washed her face, then lay down on a couch for a few minutes before dragging herself back to the table. When she returned, she saw that the lobster had been served, and the sight of it made her want to run back to the restroom. Her stomach was in violent rebellion. God, what a mess. And what could she do about it?

"Are you all right?" Brock asked, and Jenna nodded, barely able to meet his concerned gaze. "You'll be fine after you eat," he said consolingly. "We shouldn't have waited so late for dinner."

Jenna simply could not believe that this was happening. She should have been shouting for glee with Brock, but under the circumstances celebration was the last thing on her mind. "Will you order some more wine for me, please?"

"Yes, of course, but you should eat first."

She nodded, but she could actually feel her lip curl as she attempted to eat. She forced the first bite down, and the ones which followed weren't as difficult.

Somehow she suffered through the meal and managed an occasional bright smile at Brock's comments. He was really feeling like he was on his way up, but Jenna was feeling like she was on her way out. She honestly thought it would be best to tell Brock immediately what she had done, but she would wait until they went back to the house.

The dread she knew was almost unbearable, for she didn't honestly know what he would do. Would he just walk out on her again? Would he tell her that there was no way they could make a marriage, since she obviously hadn't heard a thing he had said? He had been so clear with her about achieving his career goals without her help.

She fought a hysterical urge to break into a fit of nervous giggling. My God! How they had all worked today, Jake, her band, the orchestra, herself, to make a hit of Brock's song. And he had been at another studio having it recorded for another artist! The joke was on her, of course, so why wasn't it funny?

Brock leaned across the table and stroked her arm. "Let's go to Dan's club and have a few drinks to celebrate my new career," he said, his voice husky with enthusiasm. That was the last thing Jenna wanted to do, but she nodded.

"What a wonderful idea. I want to hear the group he booked to replace me."

"But we know they won't be as good as you are," Brock told her, smiling.

"I wouldn't say that," she countered. "If I know Dan, the singer is female, good-looking, and can really perform."

Brock laughed. "You may be right. We'll find out." He left money for the check, and they walked out of the building. Jenna's legs were in a state of rebellion, but she kept putting one foot in front of the other and moving forward.

To their surprise, when they stepped out onto the sidewalk, flashbulbs went off. "Look over here, Jenna, Brock," someone called out, and Jenna recognized a familiar local reporter's voice. So tonight she and Brock were news again. Tomorrow their pictures would be plastered across the papers. And by tomorrow night—

Her smile was long-practiced, one that would hold up through good times as well as bad, and she made it work for her as she and Brock made their way through the news people. The questions were many and fast, and included some that were tactless about Brock's scars; this time Jenna was glad that Brock hadn't changed enough to hold still long enough to answer them.

"No comment," he said firmly, and his smile was the slightest bit strained.

Jenna didn't breathe easily until they were in a cab and on the way to Dan's nightclub, and even then she couldn't relax. She didn't remember the drive to the night spot. Brock didn't comment about the photographers, and neither did she. It was a way of life with a performer who was successful and visible. But Jenna could tell that Brock's mood had altered somewhat. The reporters had dampened his earlier joy by reminding him of the realities of exposing himself to the public again.

The club was packed, and Jenna searched among the people, looking for Dan. He always kept a few tables reserved; she knew he would give them one, of course. She spied him at last, and she took Brock's hand to lead him toward a table near the front but off to one side. Dan was sitting there with a tall brunette, and Jenna smiled faintly to herself. It didn't look like he was pining away over her, much to her relief.

When she approached the table, he stood up immediately and embraced her. "Jenna, how are you?" His manner with Brock was more reserved, but quite civil. They exchanged greetings, and then Dan turned to the woman at the table. "This is Joy Jefferies, a singer with the group playing tonight. Joy, Jenna and Brock Hanson."

Joy smiled winningly at them and murmured a few pleasantries before she excused herself. "We're up in five minutes," she announced. "So nice to have met you."

Jenna watched as she walked away, tall, sexy, and quite young. "That one's a beauty, Dan," she said.

"Isn't she, though?" he murmured, his eyes slightly teasing. "And single." He indicated two chairs. "Here, sit down. I'm so glad that you came."

They were barely seated when some of the regular patrons came up to talk with Jenna and to get her autograph for various relatives. Some of them remembered Brock all too well, and Jenna saw surprise in their eyes as they stared at his scars. Dan ordered drinks, and Brock leaned back in his chair and began to nurse his scotch when it arrived. Jenna was proud that he didn't seem to notice the shocked looks people gave him when they saw the scars for the first time.

Finally the house lights dimmed, and Joy and her group took their places on stage. They were very good, and the crowd loved them. Joy paid Jenna tribute by asking her to come up and sing a song with the band, and although Jenna wanted to refuse, she accepted graciously. She lightly caressed Brock's shoulder as she walked past him, and he caught her hand and brushed it with his lips.

Jenna announced that she was singing "Hold Love Tightly" and that her husband, Brock Hanson, had written it for her and was in the audience. She gazed at Brock across the heads of the other patrons as she sang, and she hoped the words he had written with her in mind made impact.

She could see a lean man approach Brock's table while she

sang, and she realized that it was Derek Jones, a member of her band. Suddenly a dreadful thing occurred to her. In her confusion and shock earlier that day she had forgotten that she wanted to swear the band to secrecy. She hadn't meant for anyone to tell Brock about her recording "When Love Is Gone." She wrapped up her song very quickly, waited only briefly to acknowledge the applause, then handed the microphone back to Joy.

By the time she had made her way back to the table, past the fans trying to shake her hand or talk to her, Brock was gone. Jenna's chest tightened until she could hardly breathe. She dropped down into a chair by Derek. "Where did he go?" she asked in a ragged, breathless voice.

Derek looked totally confused. "It was the damnedest thing," he said. "I spoke to him, and he was very friendly, but when I told him what a big hit you were going to have with that record we added to the album today, he looked like I'd slapped him in the face with the news. Without saying a word he shoved back his chair, looked at you, and walked out. Dan went after him, but I saw him come back alone. What happened? Did I do something wrong?"

Jenna clasped both hands over her mouth and struggled not to let Derek see the tears in her eyes. She shook her head, and when she could speak, she murmured, "No, you didn't. I did. That was Brock's new song I recorded today, and I didn't tell him what I was doing."

"Hell, Jenna!" Derek muttered in a low voice. "Why didn't you tell somebody? I wouldn't have messed you up for anything, but I think you're up to your pretty neck in trouble, girl."

She nodded, and her mouth twisted in bitter regret. "Don't remind me. Oh, Derek, I've got to find him and try to explain. Excuse me."

She was rushing out the door when someone grabbed her arm. She hadn't seen Brock step out from the shadows by the door, and she gasped as he stopped her.

"You scared me," she murmured.

"You'll be lucky if that's all I do to you," he said in a soft, dangerous voice. "You had no right to record that song!"

She waited until she was out on the sidewalk, and then she attempted desperately to explain. "Brock, if you'll only listen to me, I'll tell you why I did that."

She blinked when a flashbulb went off, and she turned to glare at the photographer, her long-practiced smile nowhere to be found. The news had spread fast apparently, and the photographer had followed them.

Jenna could see the headlines now: HOSTILE HANSONS BACK TOGETHER AND AT IT AGAIN. She knew the guy, and she walked over to him. "Look, Gary, I really would appreciate it if you would leave us alone now. I'll give you a scoop later if you'll just back off now."

"Promise?" he asked interestedly.

She nodded, wishing she could slap his face instead.

"Agreed."

He walked away, and when Jenna turned back, Brock was nowhere to be found. A single tear slipped down her face as she stood out on the dark street all alone. Another followed. They began to pour unchecked as she hurried toward her car, and Jenna let them fall where they might.

Brock was driving much too fast as he made his way toward Prout's Neck. Everything had been looking up—or so he had thought. Then Jenna had to go and pull a damned stunt like that. He had thought they could start on an even footing as man and wife—composer and singer—but no, that hadn't been the case at all. Jenna. Jenna. Jenna. What had she meant to do to him? Whatever it was, she had achieved it so well. The thing he had feared most—that people would think he had gone back to her to find a place for himself in the business under her umbrella—had happened. And she had caused it.

Jenna lay in her bed in Boston all alone, sobbing softly to

herself. The odds against her and Brock's living happily ever after had been too great. She had done what she had thought was best, and she had made a grave error. He hadn't even done her the courtesy of listening; he had walked out on her just as he had when he had left her before, and she would not torture herself by trying to hunt him down a second time.

Her mother had been right; she had been a fool. But she had had to try. She had loved Brock too much not to at least try. And she had failed. She had known there was a chance of that when she recorded the song, and she had known that the hurt would come again, twisting her insides and making her heart bleed with pain and regret, but she was astounded by the magnitude of her disappointment. She had been close, so close, to having everything she wanted most. But being close only caused her to hurt more.

She and she alone had ruined Brock's first effort to make himself successful. She had destroyed his delight in the demo, just as she had destroyed their newfound delight in each other. She had made the one mistake calculated to bring Brock the most grief, or so he thought: Jenna O'Neil, his wife and somehow his enemy in the music business, had recorded the song he wanted to use to make a comeback all on his own.

To her dismay she realized that they hadn't achieved as much as they had hoped on the road to a new beginning. When things had gone wrong, the first thing Brock had done was close up on her. Communication was critical, and he had not let her explain what she had done and why. She would not try again. Finally her heart accepted the futility of loving Brock. But even though it accepted, it didn't understand. Jenna rolled over on her side, curled up in a ball of wrenching misery, and sobbed long into the night.

She went about the motions of life when morning finally dragged itself into her bedroom to prod her from a restless sleep. She had several cups of coffee and a piece of buttered toast. It was almost noon before she dressed, and even then she didn't know what to do with herself. Everywhere she went in the house there were reminders of Brock and the night before.

Finally the memories chased her out; she decided to have another talk with her mother. Apparently it coincided perfectly with her mother's plans.

"I'm so pleased to see you," Joan said brightly when she saw Jenna. "I've been thinking a lot about our talk yesterday, and I confess that I feel like a weight has been lifted off my shoulders."

"I'm glad," Jenna murmured. "I thought we might have lunch. Do you already have plans?"

"No. It's a wonderful idea." They both seemed to have things they wanted to say, but neither of them spoke until they had gone to a sprawling restaurant filled with diners. Jenna needed and wanted the commotion and distraction today.

"Jenna, all those years I felt guilty about not telling you about Drummond, about you having a father who was alive, and now it's finally over. I can't help but wonder if you despise me for what I did."

Patting her mother's hand absently, Jenna realized how little difference the news made to her. Once again her primary concern was Brock and their hopeless future.

She shook her head. "I don't despise you at all, Mother. You've more than paid the price in misery. I'm only sorry you didn't tell me sooner so that your secret wouldn't have hung over your head all these years."

"What will you do about it, Jenna?" Joan's brown eyes were almost frightened.

Glancing up, Jenna looked at Joan's concerned face. "About what?"

"About Drummond being your father."

Jenna shrugged. "Nothing. The man wants his privacy, and he's welcome to it. I've never had a father, and I don't miss what I haven't had."

Jenna didn't imagine the immense relief that washed over Joan's features, but Joan quickly changed the subject. "How are

179

things with you and Brock?" She didn't wait for an answer. "Jenna, I want you to know that I realize how I've misjudged Brock. I'm going to try, really try, to be fair about him—about you two as a couple—from now on."

Averting her eyes to stare down at the silverware, Jenna fought the urge to break into tears and run to her mother's arms for comfort as she had done when she was a child. "It doesn't matter, Mother. Brock and I can't make it. It just won't work. You were right."

Joan sat in stunned silence for a moment. "What happened? Yesterday you were so positive—"

"Yesterday I was a fool," Jenna muttered. "It just won't work, that's all."

Joan's voice was sympathetic and coaxing. "Tell me what happened, please. I'd like to help if I can."

Jenna laughed bleakly. Joan was willing too late; there was nothing anyone could do. Still, her mother's sudden sympathy moved her. She needed to talk, to get it all out; then maybe she could forget. "It's an old story," she said softly. "I succeeded faster than Brock, and he had such high standards for himself. I was silly and said things I didn't mean. We were both too jealous, too possessive . . ."

She looked at Joan. "I loved him too much. I would have done anything to get him back after he left me, and when I saw that we had a chance, I was desperate to see Brock work again so that I wouldn't lose him for the same old reasons. I recorded a song he had written." She laughed bleakly and bitterly. "It was the one thing he didn't want. He wanted to make it on his own, to be my equal in the business, and I recorded his song—at great trouble and expense, I might add—on the same day he made a demo of it for his manager." Her voice cracked. "God, Mother," she murmured, her voice choked with emotion, "it seems that the harder I try with that man, the worse things get. Now it's starting all over again, the pain, the heartache, the loss. I would have been better off if I'd never seen him again."

"Oh, Jenna, I'm so sorry. I know how you must hurt. I wish I could do something to help."

"There's nothing more to be done," Jenna said. "In fact, that's the problem. Too much has already been done. I really don't want to talk about it anymore." She was so distraught that she couldn't speak at all, for now she realized how long and lonely the last eleven months had been without Brock. Just when she had been on the road to recovery, he had stepped onto her path again, and now she would go through it all a second time—only this time she had finally learned that there would be no cause for dreaming or hoping.

Joan looked thoughtfully at her daughter. "What we should do is take a trip together," she said at length.

Jenna didn't miss the ease with which her mother changed the topic, and she wondered if Joan wasn't secretly grateful that Brock had been dispensed with once again. She began to talk about the two of them going away to France, and the disturbing subject of Brock was shoved into the shadows of Jenna's consciousness, where it festered and destroyed.

For the next couple of days Jenna was thankful for her mother's idea. They shopped around for the best trip package to France, and Jenna bought some new clothes. Her passport was in order, and she began to take a real interest in traveling outside the country; it would be a good way to escape the haunting memories of Brock's second devastating intrusion into her life.

She was eager to escape the newly made and vivid memories of herself and Brock at Prout's Neck. His words rang in her ears, and she could feel his touch on her skin as surely as if he were still with her. She loved him more than ever now because she had had another taste of life with him, and it was stark and empty without him.

She asked herself a hundred times why he didn't at least call her. She sat by the phone when she was at home, waiting as though she honestly expected him to phone, but he didn't, of course. The only respite Jenna had from her haunting memories were her talks with Joan about the trip and their related excursions.

At last all the arrangements were made, and Jenna was pacing nervously about the living room, waiting for her mother to arrive. Joan had the tickets. Even though they had several hours before catching the plane, they had agreed to have lunch together before going to the airport. Joan was late, which wasn't at all like her. Jenna had tried to call her but got no answer.

The doorbell rang finally, and she raced to the door. "Mother —" she cried, flinging it open. Her words stopped suddenly when she saw Brock standing there. She gazed in stunned surprise. She had wanted to see him for so long, had dreamed of him, longed for him, mourned his loss; but she wasn't prepared to face him now. She hadn't seen or heard from him since he had disappeared three nights ago, and she had resigned herself to the fact that he was gone—again. She hadn't even let herself think about what would happen with the song she had recorded. She had needed some distance between her and that disastrous day so that she could think rationally about it.

"May I come in?"

She wanted to refuse him. God knew she wanted to tell him to go away and never approach her in any way ever again, but her heart had heard his question, and it answered for her. "Yes."

Jenna watched as he walked in, so handsome, so appealing as always, and she stood by nervously as he settled down on the couch. He seemed to be finding this as hard as she did. Had he come to tell her it was over? To threaten her? Punish her? Or was there a chance he had come to forgive her?

Her throat tightened painfully at the thought, and she searched his face for some sign of his thoughts, but there was no clue to his motive in coming here.

He met her eyes, then looked away. "Your mother came to see me," he said at last.

Jenna's brows rose involuntarily. "Joan?"

Brock nodded. "She said you had a very good reason for recording my song without my permission."

Closing her eyes briefly, Jenna sank down in the nearest chair. She didn't know if she had the strength to try to explain it all to him, and she was astonished that Joan had gone to him without telling her. She wouldn't have allowed it. If Brock had wanted her, it was his place to come to her.

She made herself look at him. "I did it for you, whether or not you believe it. For you and for us."

"I wanted to do it on my own," he said simply. "I didn't want you doing it the easy way. I didn't want people to think I'd used you to find a place for myself because I couldn't make it on my own."

"Do you think I did it the *easy* way?" she suddenly demanded. "Do you think it was easy getting that tape, convincing Wayne and Jake? Hiring an arranger on such short notice, getting the orchestra and band and the session lined up? My album was finished, but I wanted the world to know about your record. And I knew you and I had no chance at all if you didn't work again."

She looked away. "I had no way of knowing you would do something with the song yourself. You wouldn't even talk to me about it." She raised her eyes. "And what's so bad about me helping you, Brock? Don't you ever think in terms of us? You and me? I didn't have anything without you, and I knew you wouldn't be mine without a career."

"When I heard you'd recorded the song, Jenna, I was sure it meant that you felt I'd never make it without you to help."

She shook her head. "Oh, Brock, stop making things so hard on yourself—on me. Is it so wrong to accept help? Wouldn't you have done the same for me?"

Brock's eyebrows came together in a troubled frown, and Jenna knew that she had scored a point whether or not he would admit it. There was a pause as he considered her words; then he said, "Joan told me you knew you might lose me when you did it."

Jenna nodded. "I had to take the chance. I knew you'd never be happy until you worked again."

"But you risked everything. Why?"

"I love you more than I feared losing you, I guess." Her eyes met his, and she was pleading with him to understand.

"I had Jake play the song for me," Brock said softly. "You've done it much more beautifully than Austin Lane ever could have."

"Brock?" she murmured questioningly, not sure what his statement meant. "Aren't you angry?"

"I was at first, but how can I be now, when I understand why and how much trouble you went to just to help me, Jen?" He stood up and walked over to kneel down by her chair. "I love you, Jen. More than my career, more than life itself. I wanted to do things on my own so that you wouldn't lose respect for me, so that you could be proud of me. I see now that love doesn't work that way. I've been thinking about pride. We *should* be a team—you and I—helping each other."

He reached out and touched her cheek with his damaged hand. His fingers were stiff and rough against her skin, and Jenna held them to her lips to kiss them. Brock smiled at her tenderly, the love for her deep in his eyes.

"It never mattered to you at all, did it?" he asked. "The scars, the ugliness?"

"I love you, Brock. Nothing else mattered. You're beautiful to me. And will always be, no matter what."

Brock pulled some tickets from his pocket. "Here's a gift from your mother. A trip to France for a second honeymoon. We'll get away from *both* careers. It'll be a time just for you and me, Jen. A time to heal and build for the future. I know we can work it all out. We love each other too much not to." He laughed gently. "We'll be the best in the business. Hanson and O'Neil. Or is it O'Neil and Hanson?"

"It's Hanson and Hanson all the way," she told him, her love for him evident in the way she looked at him.

He moved forward to claim her mouth in a lingering kiss, and Jenna knew that this time it was forever. They would smooth the rough spots with tenderness and consideration, for there was no disharmony in their careers now. Their song was the same: that magical and beautiful song of lasting love.

LOOK FOR NEXT MONTH'S
CANDLELIGHT ECSTASY ROMANCES ®

When You Want A Little More Than Romance—

Try A Candlelight Ecstasy!

SWEET WILD WIND

by Joyce Verrette

In the primeval forests of America, passion was born in the
mystery of a stolen kiss.

A high-spirited beauty, daughter of the furrier to the French
king, Aimee Dessaline had led a sheltered life. But on one fateful
afternoon, her fate was sealed with a burning kiss. Vale's sun
bronzed skin and buckskins proclaimed his Indian upbringing,
but his words belied another heritage. Convinced that he was a
spy, she vowed to forget him—this man they called Valjean
d'Auvergne, Comte de la Tour.

But not even the glittering court at Versailles where Parisian
royalty courted her favors, not even the perils of the war torn
wilderness could still her impetuous heart.

A DELL BOOK   17634-4   ($3.95)

Seize The Dawn

by Vanessa Royall

For as long as she could remember, Elizabeth Rolfson knew that her destiny lay in America. She arrived in Chicago in 1885, the stunning heiress to a vast empire. As men of daring pressed westward, vying for the land, Elizabeth was swept into the savage struggle. Driven to learn the secret of her past, to find the one man who could still the restlessness of her heart, she would stand alone against the mighty to claim her proud birthright and grasp a dream of undying love.

A DELL BOOK   17788-X $3.50

Desert Hostage

Diane Dunaway

Behind her is England and her first innocent encounter
with love. Before her is a mysterious land of forbidding
majesty. Kidnapped, swept across the deserts of
Araby, Juliette Barclay sees her past vanish in the
endless, shifting sands. Desperate and defiant, she
seeks escape only to find harrowing danger, to
discover her one hope in the arms of her captor, the
Shiek of El Abadan. Fearless and proud, he alone can
tame her. She alone can possess his soul. Between
them lies the secret that will bind her to him forever, a
woman possessed, a slave of love.

A DELL BOOK   11963-4 $3.95

NEW DELL

CANDLELIGHT Ecstasy Supreme

LOVERS AND PRETENDERS,
by Prudence Martin
$2.50

Christine and Paul—looking for new lives on a cross-country jaunt, were bound by lies and a passion that grew more dangerously honest with each passing day. Would the truth destroy their love?

WARMED BY THE FIRE,
by Donna Kimel Vitek
$2.50

When malicious gossip forces Juliet to switch jobs from one television network to another, she swears an office romance will never threaten her career again—until she meets superstar anchorman Marc Tyner.